The *
Pillow Book
of Lotus Lowenstein ♡

The Pillow Book of Lotus Lowenstein

LIBBY SCHMAIS

delacorte press

Copyright © 2009 by Libby Schmais

All rights reserved. Published in the United States by Delacorte Press, an imprint of Random House Children's Books, a division of Random House, Inc., New York. Originally published in hardcover in the United States by Delacorte Press in 2009.

Delacorte Press is a registered trademark and the colophon is a trademark of Random House, Inc.

Visit us on the Web! www.randomhouse.com/teens
Educators and librarians, for a variety of teaching tools, visit us at www.randomhouse.com/teachers

The Library of Congress has cataloged the hardcover edition of this work as follows:
Schmais, Libby.
The pillow book of Lotus Lowenstein / Libby Schmais.
p. cm.
Summary: Quirky sixteen-year-old Lotus Lowenstein's diary reveals that although she lives in Brooklyn and is failing high school French, she loves all things Gallic and dreams of living as an existentialist in Paris.
ISBN 978-0-385-73756-2 (hardcover) — ISBN 978-0-385-90673-9 (lib. bdg.) —
ISBN 978-0-375-89380-3 (e-book)
[1. Individuality—Fiction. 2. High schools—Fiction. 3. Schools—Fiction. 4. Diaries—Fiction. 5. France—Fiction. 6. Family life—New York (State)—New York—Fiction. 7. Brooklyn (New York, N.Y.)—Fiction. 8. Humorous stories.] I. Title.
PZ7.S3473Pi 2009
[Fic]—dc22
2008043526

ISBN 978-0-385-73757-9 (tr. pbk.)

Printed in the United States of America

10 9 8 7 6 5 4 3 2 1

First Trade Paperback Edition

Random House Children's Books supports the First Amendment and celebrates the right to read.

To Sam, avec beaucoup de love

ACKNOWLEDGMENTS

I would like to thank my family and friends for encouraging me in the writing of this book, with special thanks to Beth, Debbie, and Sam for their endless readings and helpful advice. I'd also like to express my gratitude to Mr. Aschmann, for his help early on in my writing life. A big *merci* goes to Mina for our writing dates, which were invaluable. I also sincerely thank my agent, Stephen Barbara, and my editor, Stephanie Elliott, for their belief in this book.

The
Pillow Book
of Lotus Lowenstein

one

Lundi, 12 Mars

As you may have guessed, my name is Lotus Lowenstein and this is my diary. My name is not a joke; it actually says Lotus on my birth certificate. My mother was into some whole Zen/yoga thing when I was born. I'm sixteen (almost) and I'm in the middle of my sophomore year in high school, and I know that this year will be completely different than all other years of my life. This year, I will become an existentialist, go to France, and fall in love (hopefully in Paris) with a dashing Frenchman named

Jean-something. We will both be existentialists, believe in nothingness, and wander around Paris in trench coats and berets.

There are obstacles to my plan. Just this morning, my mother informed me that there was no way I was going to France this summer, because of economics. It's ridiculous. What are family economics compared to my development as an existentialist? It's not like they don't have enough money when they want to—for example, when their favorite child, my little brother, Adam, needs a new laptop to practice chess simulations. Oh, did I mention that my brother is some kind of chess genius?

"My life is *merde*," I told my mother. "*Merde*, do you hear me?"

"The whole Northeast hears you, Lotus."

"I must go to Paris!"

"We can't afford it right now, honey. You know your brother needs a new laptop, and if you haven't noticed, the roof is in desperate need of repairs. And your father is between careers, so . . . to each according to their need, as Karl Marx would say, and you don't need, emphasis *need*, to go to Paris right now."

"But I do—I will die if I don't."

"No you won't. You'll be fine. You'll finish high school. Take the SAT, go to college. Have a fulfilling career."

"Like you, Maman?"

My mother kept chopping carrots into little pieces, as if they were the enemy. My mother has been especially irritable lately. She claims she is going through early menopause and insists on telling me about it, in the interests of mother-daughter bonding, although if we haven't bonded by now, I fear it's a little too late.

I recommended French homeopathic remedies to her, but all she wanted to do was complain. When she started talking about vaginal dryness and how someday this would happen to me, I put my hands over my ears and yelled, "Too much information!" until she stopped.

It is *très* difficult being me. I am trapped in a crumbling *maison* in Park Slope, Brooklyn, with crazy people who claim to be related to me. They insist on dinner every night at the unfashionable hour of six-thirty, like we are farmhands. How am I supposed to develop a chic figure if I am forced to eat this starchy American food? *Mon Dieu*, we don't even have a cheese course! Not that I'm *grosse* (fat), but I'm not *mince* (thin), either. My friend Joni says I'm curvy and that she'd love to have my figure. I do like the way I look for the most part. I'm a brunette, like most French women, and I have a *frange* (bangs) and a unique sense of style. But I do think that if I lost a few *kilos*, I'd probably look better in haute couture.

Mes parents scoff at all my ideas, but it's not like they seem particularly happy about the boring way we do things now. When I told my mother that I was thinking of becoming a *catholique*, because everyone in France is *catholique*, her response was a groan and "Lotus, are you kidding me?"

School (sigh):

At nine o'clock in the morning—a little early for me—

I was in English (advanced placement, can you believe it?). Ms. G, my teacher, is nice, though kind of tragic, I guess, because she lives alone and must be at least forty. If she were in France, she could be a mysterious older woman like Juliette Binoche or Isabelle Adjani, but here she's merely old and invisible. It's not that she wears horrible clothes, it's just that her clothes don't make enough of a statement. She needs scarves, accessories, more makeup, better hair. Her shoes scream comfortable (the kiss of death), and the drab colors she wears (black, black, and more black) don't scream anything, they just whimper in the background. Black is chic on a younger woman like *moi*, but a femme of a certain age, well, she needs a little color.

DIARIES, Ms. G wrote on the board in big block letters, and I felt a frisson. (*Frisson* is also French, for shiver of excitement.) I had the frisson because I am all about diaries: I've been keeping a journal religiously for several years. My personal diary is not ready to be revealed to *le monde* (the world) yet, but I am still psyched to study the diary format, since it will help me perfect my craft.

In fact, I can see the future already. I will publish my diary and it will be a huge success, a phenomenon. I'll be a teen sensation, bigger than Bridget Jones, bigger than John Lennon and the Dalai Lama, bigger than Lindsay Lohan. I am debating whether to call my oeuvre *The Pillow Book of Lotus Lowenstein* or *Pensées of Lotus Lowenstein*. *Pensées* are deep thoughts, in case you were wondering. I decided to ask Ms. G her opinion. She's a good teacher, most of the time. I'm contemplating dedicating my book to her. Despite her brutal critiques, I feel she truly understands me.

Mardi, 13 Mars

Our first assignment is based on the diary of Sei Shōnagon, a lady-in-waiting to the Japanese court in 990, about a gazillion years ago. She started writing her pillow book because someone gave her a pillowcase full of paper, how random is that? She wrote lists of things she liked and didn't like and talked about stuff that happened to her. Our homework is to write diary entries about our lives, à la Sei Shōnagon.

Assignment #1
Adorable Things

Duck eggs
An urn containing the relics of some holy person.
Wild pinks
—Sei Shōnagon

Things J'adore

French men (although I haven't met any, I'm sure they would be charmant and we would drink many espressos and have mad, passionate affairs). I am a great believer in l'amour. Did I mention I am also an existentialist like Simone de Beauvoir, except she was bisexual and outdoorsy and I don't think I am bisexual and I am definitely not outdoorsy.

J'adore my dog, Rags, whom I've renamed Pierre le chien (Pierre the dog). He is the only member of my

*family who does not condescend to me. Pierre is a mutt,
but I feel that he has some purebred chien in him.*

*Vintage clothes—they look better on me than the insipid
fashions of this time period.*

*Café, which is incredibly delicious. My father has been
letting me have café au laits from the espresso machine I
bought him for winter solstice (we're Jewish, but we
don't believe in organized religion). I always put in lots of
steamed milk, four sugars, and some powdered chocolate. C'est merveilleux.*

—Lotus Lowenstein

*P.S. Have you ever thought of getting a makeover,
Ms. G? I think you'd be hot—I mean, très chic.*

Ms. Lowenstein,
    While I applaud your creative use of the
diary format and your budding knowledge of
French, I would greatly appreciate it if you
would restrict yourself to the subject as-
signed and the requested word count. Also,
please insert quotes from The Pillow Book.
Ms. G
Good effort overall!

two

Sat in Barnes & Noble after school reading *French Women Don't Get Fat,* by Mireille Guiliano. It is a brilliant book. I feel as if the author is speaking directly to me. It is my crass American lifestyle that is responsible for this pudge around my waist. I should sue the government for what they've done to me.

I went to the Union Market to buy leeks, yogurt, and dark chocolate. Leeks are a magical food according to Mireille, and I am planning to make the special leek broth

7

from her book. My mother gave me money to buy organic chicken, couscous, and squash, but I'm not sure she understands anything about nutrition. If I eat like the average French woman, I will be svelte. I really need champagne to make this diet—excuse me, this lifestyle—work, but I'm not sure I can swing champagne on what she gave me and without a forged ID.

Assignment #2
Things Je Déteste

One is in a hurry to leave, but one's visitor keeps chattering away. . . .
—*Sei Shōnagon*

I totally related to that, like when I'm trying to leave in the morning and I'm late for school and my dad will want to chat with me about MY LIFE and how things are going.

Je déteste gym. The "popular" girls like to show off their bodies by wearing the tightest gym clothes possible and are always trying to do splits. Personally, I think walking in high heels on cobblestones is the only exercise I will ever need, not that it is offered as part of the curriculum.

Je déteste knitting. It's ridiculous. All these hipster girls are doing it during lunch and they mistakenly think it's cool. I mean, why not leave the knitting of scarves to the people who know how to do it instead of having to wear lumpy handmade stuff? Plus, it is important to support the artisanal worker—like my mother gives money to support some microworkers in Indonesia who make scarves. Knit scarves are not my style, but I don't think we should take away the artisanals' livelihood and impoverish them further.

Je déteste other girls—they are mean and stupide. Except Joni, of course, who is my closest friend and totally understands me and my fashion sense. But other girls, that's a different histoire. Like the other day, I was wearing an Hermès scarf (or at least that's what the woman at Gently Used told me) wrapped around my shoulders in a French style à la Catherine Deneuve, the incredibly beautiful and chic French movie star, and this gaggle of popular girls, the same ones who do splits in gym, were giggling and pointing at me when I went by. Joni said they were just jealous. It's très important to have a loyal friend, especially when you are surrounded by such cretins.

Je déteste school. It's hideous and unnecessary. I don't understand math or science. I am a right-brain person and shouldn't be subjected to these archaic requirements. I'm supposed to be studying for the SAT, but I don't even care about them. I'm going to be a foreign correspondent and I don't think I need college for that.

—Lotus Lowenstein

Ms. Lowenstein,

I enjoyed reading your latest diary entry. High school is a challenging time.

I'm glad you're thinking about your future, but try not to neglect math and science. They may seem irrelevant right now, but they will come in handy later.

Ms. G

three

Jeudi, 15 Mars

For social studies, our assignment is to watch the news, pick a program, and report on it. Everyone else is doing CNN or network news, so I decided to choose something from the E! network. As a journalist, I think it's very important to be up on popular culture.

Joni TiVo'd an E! *True Hollywood Story* on Angelina Jolie for me, because *mes parents* only let us record shows from PBS and the Discovery Channel. Watching it, I learned so much. In 2005, Angelina Jolie had an affair with Brad Pitt and then he and Jennifer Aniston broke up. After that, Brad and

Angelina moved in together and adopted about a dozen children. They also had three of their own. I didn't see what the big deal was. People in France have affairs all the time, and the couples live happily ever after without all this divorce and pregnancy. What Angelina should have done is just had an affair and then given Brad back to Jennifer Aniston, who seemed like a more stable person. Didn't Angelina have a French mother, after all? And what's this obsession with having children? They don't seem very interesting to me, and what they do to your body, *mon Dieu*, let's not even think about that.

My *grand-mère* was at my house when I got home from Barnes & Noble. My grandmother is one of those purple hat, red dress ladies. Or is it purple dress, red hat ladies? I forget. Anyway, all these old-lady friends of hers get together and have this club, which mostly involves drinking at Applebee's as far as I can tell. It's a nationwide phenomenon, and apparently, they have some kind of rule book that tells them what to do.

When my *grand-mère* described the red hat ladies to us, my mother just rolled her eyes, but I thought it was kind of cool. I mean, by that age, all the men have basically died off, so it's nice to have something to occupy your time. My *mère* and my *grand-mère* don't get along. They both think they know the right way to do everything, even if it's just chopping an onion. My mother uses a giant Henckels knife and hacks away, but my grandmother uses a tiny paring knife and slowly chops the onion into tiny pieces.

"You should be using shallots anyway," I said, in an attempt to defuse the tension. "They have more panache than onions."

"She's obsessed with France," my mom said to my grandmother, raising her unplucked eyebrows.

"I think that's wonderful," said my grandmother, giving me a squeeze. "If you had continued your studies, Cynthia, you could have been a doctor."

"Mom, my name is Suki."

"I know you've insisted on calling yourself that ridiculous name ever since you were in that cult, but your name is Cynthia. I can show you your birth certificate if you like."

"It wasn't a cult, it was a Buddhist meditation group, and by the way, Suki is Japanese and it means 'beloved.' "

"Well, Cynthia is American and it means you were named after your great-aunt Cynthia, may God rest her soul."

"Mom, you are a . . ." Luckily, at this moment my mother cut her finger, and we all had to hunt for Band-Aids. The argument was forgotten.

After dinner, I went over to Joni's to study like I do most days. Joni has been my best friend forever. We met in third grade during lunch, when she swapped her peanut butter sandwich and chocolate cookies for my boring hummus and carrots. We soon discovered we both had Hello Kitty pencil cases and an obsession with Bratz dolls, although I wasn't allowed to have any—my mother said they looked like baby hookers—so Joni invited me over to play with hers. Since then, we've been inseparable.

Joni has a much bigger, more luxurious house than we do, and better food. Weeks have gone by where I only ate dinner at Joni's and my parents would start to make jokes about whether her family was planning on adopting me. Today, Joni's mom made quesadillas for us and virgin margaritas.

My mom says Joni's mom is a Stepford wife because she always looks so perfect, but I like her. Joni's mom (Julia, she tells me to call her) and Joni's dad met at a John Sebastian concert in Central Park in the Pleistocene era. They were totally into that old, folky kind of music, although now all they listen to is classical. Joni's mom told her that she was named after Joni Mitchell because that's who was on the radio when she was conceived. I think that's kind of cool and kind of creepy at the same time. Sometimes, Joni and I play her parents' old records and dance around. Joni thinks the Joni Mitchell song that was playing while they did it was "Little Green," but I think it was probably "A Case of You."

We did our homework, only taking short breaks to read old *People* magazines. I started reading an article about Sheryl Crow. She's very political and even adopted a baby a couple of years ago. I find it interesting that right after she broke up with Lance Armstrong, she got breast cancer. I wonder if there was a connection. Was she just so devastated after they broke up that her immune system couldn't fight it off? In science class, Mr. Higgleston told us that we all have cancer cells circulating in our bodies at all times but only in certain people do they become actual cancer. Everyone was freaked out by this, and a couple of girls said they were going to quit smoking the next day. I never thought Lance Armstrong was so great anyway, although everyone else seems to think he's some kind of superhero. I mean, there are a lot of ordinary people who get cancer—like my grandfather. The only exercise he ever did was walk their poodle, Tiny, around the block and wrestle the remote from my grandmother, but that doesn't mean he wasn't a hero.

Joe Malone, a soccer player, asked if biking gave Lance cancer of the balls. Then everyone cracked up at the word *balls*. High school students are so juvenile. Then Mr. Higgleston said, "No, there is no known connection, although biking *is* known to put a strain on the scrotal area," and everyone cracked up again. I wasn't exactly sure what a scrotal is, but I tried to look like I did.

"Hey, Joni, what do you think about Lance Armstrong?" I asked now.

"He's amazing, why?"

"Just checking."

"Do you know what a scrotal is?"

"You mean scrotum—it's the sac where the testicles are. It's basic biology."

"Right, I forgot." Why do all sex words sound so squishy and disgusting: *scrotum*, *balls*, *vagina*? Yech! I studied my French homework while Joni did her advanced placement Spanish. I don't know why she chooses to study Spanish. No one speaks it, while French is spoken everywhere in the civilized world. You'd think that I would be doing great in French, given how much I love it, but the way they teach French is so structured—verbs, nouns, conjugation—it just doesn't work for me. I need total immersion: food, clothes, wine.

"Joni, I wish I could go to Paris. I really need to go. Maybe I could rob a bank or something."

"Great idea, Lotus. I could visit you in jail and bake you a cake with a metal file and some perfume inside it."

"You'd do that for me?"

"Of course."

"But I couldn't deal with that whole bathroom-in-the-cell thing."

"Have you saved any money from your allowance or anything?" Joni asked.

"Are you kidding? I'm already three weeks in overdraft"—that's my father's term—"from buying *French Women Don't Get Fat* and my new scarf. If I ever do save enough money, I'm planning on getting some Crème de la Mer, that French face cream that makes women look beautiful."

"You're insane, it's just seaweed and water. My mother has some and I analyzed the ingredients for science class."

"Wow. You're like Madame Curie."

"Do you want to try it now?"

"Sure."

We snuck into her mom's bathroom, which was huge and marble and incredibly clean. There were dozens of vitamin bottles, potions, and natural skin products lined up precisely on the sparkling glass shelves. Joni handed me the jar of Crème de la Mer and I rubbed some on my face.

"Okay, what do you think?" I said, posing in front of the mirror.

Joni peered intently at me. "You look exactly the same."

"Thanks, you just saved me two hundred dollars."

We went back into Joni's room.

"There has to be another way to get this money for Paris besides resorting to crime," I said.

"I could lend you some."

"No, but *merci* anyway."

I wish I hadn't brought up my lack of money with Joni, because she has a lot of it and always tries to lend it to me.

Her grandparents made tons of money from some gift-basket business they started and she has a trust fund that will pay her loads of money when she's twenty-one. I don't usually take Joni up on her offers, because if I borrow money, I don't know when I'd be able to pay it back and then I would feel funny about buying stuff around her. It's weird, but Joni spends much less money than I do. Her mother always wants to take her shopping, but Joni is afraid that she will buy pink Lilly Pulitzer clothing and pants with weird swirling patterns. Joni mostly wears jeans and oversized sweaters, and occasionally overalls, which I try to talk her out of because they are so wrong. It's like she doesn't want anyone to know she has a body.

Vendredi, 16 Mars

My mother left me the ingredients for what she calls a "heart-healthy breakfast," meaning that she thinks I need to lose weight.

The breakfast was disgusting and included:

Cereal that had the consistency of cardboard

A banana (boring)

Herbal tea (I think not)

I dumped the cereal and banana in the trash can, then dragged the heavy cappuccino machine out from the cabinet above the sink and tried to remember the proportions of coffee and water. I considered asking my father, but he was probably still asleep. He lost his job as a management consultant a few years ago and has decided to permanently unchain himself from the corporate machine and write a famous play. I can't wait to see it on Broadway and tell everyone I know. According to Papa, it's a philosophical thriller. I really want to read it, but he doesn't let anyone read his work in progress, because that ruins it. I adore having a creative father, but Maman is not very supportive, probably because she had to go back to work full-time and doesn't have any time to do pottery anymore, although if you've seen her pottery you might not think that is such a bad thing.

That's what they were fighting about last night: her pottery. I had to turn up my Edith Piaf CD (my brother calls her Edith Pilaf) to drown them out. Nevertheless, I heard the crash when my dad broke my mom's favorite giant, mud-colored mug and she said he didn't care about her art and he said pottery didn't count as fine art and then she went ballistic and called him lazy and yelled something about how he wasn't supporting his family and how I wouldn't be able to go to college (like I care) and then he called her a bourgeois hypocrite and something else broke and he stalked off to his study. "Sure, go ahead and walk away, that will be real helpful," my mother yelled after him.

So, I got a horrible night's sleep after all the disturbances and it was their fault I was late for school. I gave up on the cappuccino and just grabbed the rest of the Brie and the baguette I had bought and headed off. When I got in late to first period, Ms. G said loudly, "Lotus, glad you could join us," and I realized I had forgotten my homework. *Merde.* The rest of the day was just as annoying.

When I got home from school, my father was sitting at the kitchen table reading the *Utne Reader*. He said he had a headache, so I brought him two aspirin and made some espresso, after he told me how.

"Thanks, Lotus, you're an angel."

I spooned up sugary froth from my cappuccino. "How's the play going?"

My father downed his espresso. "Still in an incubatory phase. How's school?"

"Tedious."

My father put his head in his hands and moaned.

"Dad, are you okay?"

"Whatever you do, Lotus, don't become an artist."

Later, while I was doing my social studies homework on atrocities, I had a brilliant idea. I would get a job. Yes, I would get a job, gain valuable skills, and make all the money I needed for the trip to Paris and more. There were so many jobs that I would be good at, it was hard for me to choose. I wrote down all my ideas and possible job titles, and it turned out I like a lot of the -ist jobs, such as stylist, publicist, journalist.

Journalist was my favorite. I could see myself in a trench coat (like Christiane Amanpour, but younger and more glamorous), reporting from a war-torn country, but totally safe, maybe with a couple of cute foreign bodyguards around me. It would be great to find a part-time job that would prepare me for this kind of reporting, but I wasn't sure if there was anything to report on in Park Slope, Brooklyn, except for whether it was okay to breast-feed or not in Barnes & Noble, which was a big debate in the local blogosphere. My answer on that issue is that it should be okay—I mean, it is a free country and all—but I don't want to watch it.

Lundi, 19 Mars

Today, my mother didn't fix me a heart-healthy break-fast. In fact, there was very little food at all in the whole re-frigerator. And, instead of being at work, she was lying on her yoga mat on the living-room floor. I asked if her back was hurting and she nodded. I brought her a heating pad, which I had warmed up in the microwave.

"Thanks, Lotus, I know I'm a bad mother."

"Yes, you are. You won't let me go to Paris and there's no food. But that's okay because I'm going to get a job."

"Lotus, could you get me my emu cream from the bed-room?"

"Yes, Mom." As I rubbed the cream from aboriginal emus on her neck, I knew how slaves must have felt.

Mardi, 20 Mars

This working thing is not so bad. Yesterday was the first day of my new job.

I wore an old purple and yellow Betsey Johnson dress of my mother's (which was just a little tight around the hips), pink fishnet stockings, and my white and blue Tyrolean coat. As I was leaving the house, my father said I looked like a demented Heidi, but what does he know about fashion? He's always wearing the same Grateful Dead T-shirt and old sweatpants.

I got the job because of my mother's bad back. I went with her to the chiropractor the other day and we chatted with Barbara, the office manager and on-call doula. She's tall and wears long African dresses and has tight blond dreadlocks. I asked her what a doula was, and she went into a tedious explanation, saying a doula is sort of a cross between a midwife and a cheerleader. Then my mother and Barbara got into a really graphic discussion of vaginas and menopause and I tuned them out until Barbara said they were looking for a part-time receptionist. I perked up at this and started kicking my mother lightly to get her attention, but she just pushed my foot aside and kept talking. Finally, I coughed and said, "What about me? I could do it after school and on the weekends." And my mother looked like it was the first time she had heard about me getting a job, even though I'd been talking about it forever.

"Honey, I didn't know you were interested in a job."

"Don't you remember? I told you. Oh, forget it."

"I didn't know you were serious. Well, I *guess* you could handle it," she said doubtfully.

"Well, if you are serious, Lotus, we could really use you," said Barbara. Voilà, I got my first job!

I love my desk at the Wellness Center. I arranged everything twice: my phone, my message pad, the pile of blank insurance forms I give people to fill out, and my basket of individually wrapped lavender aromatherapy wipes. Barbara is super nice and friendly, although she did ask me not to answer the phone with *"Bonjour."* Instead, I'm supposed to say, "Hello, I'm Lotus. Welcome to the Wellness Center, a holistic healing environment. How can I assist you in your healing journey?" Personally, I think people like a little continental flair, but she said they would think they got a wrong number.

When I sat down at my new desk, there were already a bunch of people in the waiting room, reading *Organic Style* and *Yoga Journal*. There was also a woman lugging a baby around the room trying to teach it stuff, although the baby seemed totally uninterested. Mothers always get this fake tone in their voice and start telling their kids random facts they don't care about, like, "Look, honey, this is bamboo. It's a symbol of good luck." The kids are going to have more than enough homework soon enough, so why don't their mothers just leave them alone, or teach them something important, like how to accessorize or stop global warming?

According to my research, Sei Shōnagon wasn't big on babies either. Here's what she wrote in *The Pillow Book* about them:

Embarrassing Things

Parents, convinced that their ugly child is adorable, pet him and repeat the things he has said, imitating his voice.
—Sei Shōnagon

Aside from all the parental units, the center was pretty cool. There was a chiropractor, an acupuncturist, a Reiki practitioner, a massage therapist, a homeopath, and several other people who wandered around all day. Everyone talked in whispers and drank a lot of herbal tea. Mostly, patients called and asked about their insurance or wanted to know details about the services. When new patients came in, I had to make them fill out a bunch of forms, and I offered everyone in the waiting room our special healing tea. I tried some, but it tasted like bark, not that I've ever eaten bark. I had brought in a Starbucks latte, but Barbara made me transfer it to a mug that said TRANQUILITY because caffeine was not something the center wanted to promote. She was also not too crazy about the Starbucks corporate culture and how it disenfranchised local coffee shops, blah blah blah. I said that they are not all bad—they promote music and sell fair-trade coffee and sometimes you just really need a latte.

I tried to do homework between patients, but I couldn't focus. At home, I usually do my homework listening to music, but I'm not allowed to listen to my iPod here, which is unfair, since it would only be humane to drown out the weird chanting and drumming sounds that are piped into the waiting room. They're probably brainwashing me. In a few days, I'll wake up and want to wear some burlap-sack clothes like Barbara and drink tea made of old twigs.

The waiting room was full of moms and moms-to-be, all getting acupuncture and Reiki so they could have more children. One of the moms was doing "Itsy-Bitsy Spider" and waving her arms around like a crazy person. Her kid looked like he wished he had a choice of parents. When Barbara came by and asked for the phone messages, she picked up my ugly woven pencil case and put it back in its original spot, and also moved my stapler back to where it was before.

"The desk has been feng shuied, Lotus, so it's important to keep everything exactly where it was placed."

Whatever.

The acupuncturist came by and looked at my tongue and said I was full of vigor. I didn't mention that I'd already had three cups of coffee. She said her name was Andrea and I said mine was Lotus.

"Lotus, what a beautiful name, it means—"

"I'm named after the British sports car, actually," I said, before she went into a whole rant about how my name means birth and dawn and good fortune. It wasn't exactly true, but at least it made her stop talking.

Assignment #3
Rare Things

When people, whether they be men or women or priests, have promised each other eternal friendship, it is rare for them to stay on good terms until the end.
—Sei Shōnagon

People who can talk to you without spewing a whole bunch of factoids, like about childbirth or what your name means or how high heels throw out your back. (I didn't ask the Reiki practitioner her opinion, but if she wants mine, Birkenstocks are not cool, and wearing your hair down to your waist is just weird at any age.)

Really delicious foods that aren't fattening. I've tried to eat low-fat cheese, but it tastes disgusting and doesn't melt well. For lunch, I've been faithfully following my French diet (today I had a pain au chocolat for breakfast and Camembert and asparagus for lunch).

Incredibly Annoying Things

People who sigh, loudly, like this tedious woman who works in the office, Sheila. She does billing and administrative

stuff. Her desk is nowhere near mine, but I can hear her sighing all the way out here. She wears weird secretary clothes and clogs, but not in a cool, retro, Maggie Gyllenhaal kind of way. She also has stringy brown hair that is a crime. I've tried to be friendly with her, but her sighs are driving me mental. She has a whole bunch of sighs: long, moany sighs that would be sexual except if you saw her; gulpy, belchy sighs; and loud, sad sighs that make me want to scream. She's also the kind of person who pops up like a jack-in-the-box each time someone asks me a question that I'm perfectly capable of answering myself.
—Lotus Lowenstein

Between doing my homework and answering the phone, I tried to figure out if it was humanly possible to earn enough money with this job to go on the Paris trip.

Since I'm making ten dollars an hour, and I plan on working at least fifteen hours a week, I should be able to save one hundred fifty dollars a week, and so, in three months, I'll have eighteen hundred dollars. Wow. Maybe I can buy some vintage couture in Paris.

But first, I needed to figure out what my expenses would be in Paris.

Hotel: $80 a night (although I definitely do not want to stay in a disgusting youth hostel and sleep in the same room with Ugly Americans)
Airfare: $500 (check on this)
Cappuccinos: $4 x 3 a day

Lunch: $5 a day (baguette and cheese)
French classes: $? (check online)
French Metro card: $?
Cool French outfits: $?
Drinks: paid for by my new boyfriend, Jean-Louis or Jean-Jacques or Jean-Marc

Even if I worked three days a week after school and on Saturdays, I wasn't sure I'd have any money left to buy a lot of clothes or to eat. *Merde.* And buying all this French food here in Brooklyn is expensive. Maybe I could convince my mother to go on the French diet too, although I doubt it because she is lactose intolerant and doesn't eat bread unless it has a bunch of nuts and seeds in it.

Lundi, 26 Mars

Got back my French quiz. I got a D. This is impossible. *Quelle horreur.* French is my subject, my raison d'être—how can this be? Luckily, the parental units don't know about the quiz. I begged Mme LeFèvre to let me retake it.

She was reluctant at first, but after I begged and pretended to cry, she said, *"D'accord, mais c'est la dernière fois, Lotus."* (Translation: Okay, but it's the last time.)

I vowed to study all night for my makeup exam.

Mardi, 27 Mars

Joni and I studied all last night. She worked on her advanced placement biology and I tried to understand

French verbs and tenses. We were also watching a makeover show, which helps relax me when I study. What I learned last night is to always put your concealer on over your foundation and never wear tapered pants. Joni has a television in her room, which I think is really important, although I suspect that when I'm not there she only watches Discovery Channel or the SciFi Channel. My parents believe television rots your brain, so we're only allowed to record movies with a message and aren't allowed to have TVs in our rooms. It's ridiculous. Joni has a television and she still gets all As. My parents also don't believe in kids having cell phones, which makes my social life incredibly difficult since I can't communicate with anyone.

Example of really boring French homework:

"The rules of agreement for verbs of perception in the compound tenses are a bit different than for other verbs. Rather than agreeing with the direct object, as for most verbs conjugated with *avoir* in the compound tenses, verbs of perception only require agreement when the subject precedes the verb."

I saw the girl fall.
J'ai vu tomber la fille.
La fille que j'ai vue tomber.
Je l'ai vue tomber.

How the hell do I know which one is correct? Why is it always a girl who falls?

Mercredi, 28 Mars

I had a meeting with our school guidance counselor, Ms. Quinn. She looked at me in a very disapproving way and said I needed to have more activities on my record if I ever wanted to get into college—especially with my grades, which are mediocre at best.

"Fine," I said, "I'll join the French club."

"Lotus, you know that we don't have language clubs at this school."

Je m'en fous. I didn't care—I was going to start a French club.

I went to work again. Wore my Jacques Brel T-shirt and black beret. Sheila was driving me crazy. I was so bored I decided to keep track of how often she made weird noises.

3:35 LOUD sneeze with *dégueulasse* blowing of nose (translation: gross).

3:40 Loud yown (cross between yawn and moan). I wonder how they say *yawn* in French—I need one of those little electronic dictionaries.

3:42 Yawn plus sighing and muttering.

3:43 Small yawn.

4:00 V. loud yown.

4:10 Small belch (yech).

4:15 The phone rang and someone asked me about reflexology. I said we didn't offer it and Sheila yelled out from her cubicle that the massage therapists could do it by special request. I had to put the lady on hold because I couldn't hear what she was saying over Sheila's interrupting. When I hung up the phone, Sheila had done her popping-up thing and was standing over me waving a *Welcome to Wellness* brochure in my face and showing me where it said in a tiny footnote that reflexology was available.

"Thanks," I said, but she still wouldn't leave. She kept yammering away about how she was going to be making some kind of bean casserole that had lots of fiber for dinner from a recipe she got on the Internet and how she had a Crock-Pot and irritable bowel syndrome (too much information) and was trying to eat healthier. I just nodded, but she wouldn't go away, so I got up and pretended I had to go to the bathroom.

Sheila finally went back to her desk. "Anytime you need help, just holler."

As if.

I was reprimanded by Barbara twice today. Once for eating chocolate at my desk, and the second time for telling a pregnant woman that women in France drink during their entire pregnancies.

Well, it's true.

Later that night:

Dinner was the usual family-bonding experience. My dad made chili, which was okay, if you like a killer amount of chilies and don't mind never being able to use your taste buds again. Only after I put an enormous amount of shredded cheese and sour cream on the chili was I even able to swallow it. My father said that chilies are good for you because of the capsaicin, whatever that is. We all drank many glasses of water and I asked my parents if I could have some of their New Zealand sauvignon blanc to soothe my burning throat and they said no. I will never receive adequate nutrition or decent wine in *ma maison*.

While we were scalding our mouths with my father's chili, we had to hear all about my brother's exploits in chess club. (Despite his utter geekdom, Adam still manages to have friends and be popular, and he even makes extra money for playing with some weird old chess guys in Washington Square Park.) I tried to tell them about what happened at my job and how I was going to create a French club, but no one was listening.

My father went into some long, boring monologue about Descartes and hyperbolic doubt and how he wanted to weave it into his play and my mother said that he should be careful and not write some *Waiting for Godot* rip-off. My brother chimed in about math and Descartes and I realized how I am so not up on French philosophers and I thought about the name Descartes. Since *carte* in French means "map," I wondered if his name meant "The Maps," which was kind of *intéressant*. I mentioned this, and then everyone laughed, as if I had made a joke.

Then my father got mad at my mother and they did the not-speaking-directly-to-each-other thing. The way this works is that my mother and father take turns asking me and my brother questions, and if they want to ask each other something, they make us repeat it.

"Lotus, could you ask your father to clear the table?"

"Dad, Mom wants you to clear the table."

"Lotus, could you ask your mother to remember that I made dinner, so I am not responsible for cleanup?"

I turned to my father. "Mom, what Dad said."

"Lotus, could you remind your father that I have a bad back and am not supposed to stand for long periods of time?"

After a few minutes of this juvenile behavior, they stalked off to their respective hiding places, my dad to his office, my mother to the bathroom, and I ended up doing the dishes (my brother had to study for a chess tournament). I thought about calling the American Civil Liberties Union to lodge a complaint about my treatment, but figured they would be gone for the night.

Jeudi, 29 Mars

I told Mme LeFèvre that I wanted to start a French club.

"*Quelle bonne idée*, Lotus. You will, *bien sûr*, need to get a faculty advisor. I, unfortunately, have too much on my plate this semester, what with the de Gaulle book I am writing and my classes, *alors* . . ."

"*C'est dommage.*"

"Yes, it is too bad, Lotus, but *c'est la vie*, that's life."

Mme LeFèvre put on her reading glasses. "Here's a quote from Le Général himself. Oh, he was such a brilliant man, Lotus, a true original. I will translate for you. He said, 'How can anyone govern a nation that has two hundred forty-six different kinds of cheese?' "

"That's so true, Madame." I almost laughed, picturing someone trying to govern two hundred forty-six different kinds of cheese, but I pulled it together because Mme LeFèvre has *absolument* no sense of humor.

"*Au revoir*, Madame LeFèvre."

"*Au revoir*, Lotus. *Vive la France!*"

I wasn't going to let my lack of a faculty advisor stop me from starting a French club. I decided to have the first meeting in a week, so I'd have a chance to put up flyers and drum up interest. I told Joni she had to join. She's such a brainiac that she could learn French in a couple of days.

Vendredi, 30 Mars

I put up ten flyers around school. So far, no response, although three of the flyers were defaced with pornographic drawings and I had to take them down.

Mercredi, 4 Avril

We had our first French club meeting.
Attendees:
1. Joni
2. *Moi*

We took attendance and then decided who would be the president and who would be the vice president and secretary. I wanted to be the president because the whole thing was my idea, but Joni said she didn't want to be a secretary because it was demeaning. As we were arguing about this, a guy came into the room. I had seen him around, but I didn't know his name. He was wearing an old black motorcycle jacket and sunglasses. He was cute, in a floppy-haired, artistic kind of way. I figured he was in the wrong room.

"Hey, I'm Sean," he said, pushing his dirty-blond hair out of his face.

Joni was speechless for once, so I had to take over.

"Hi, Sean. I'm Lotus and this is Joni. This is French club, were you looking for photography club?"

"No, I'm here for French club." He sunk into a chair.

"Great." I was suspicious. Was he spying on us for the faculty?

Joni was just staring at him like a zombie, so I said, "Well, I'm the president and Joni's the vice president, so I guess you could be the treasurer." I figured we could do without a secretary.

"Cool."

It turned out that Sean was a recent transfer to our school. Joni said later he probably hadn't had time to realize how uncool French club was or how unpopular we are.

"We are not unpopular," I told her. "We are just undiscovered."

It turned out that the reason Sean wanted to be in our club is that he is obsessed with the French actress Julie Delpy. She was in that Ethan Hawke movie *Before Sunrise* where they talk all night and it's very romantic.

We're going to have a movie viewing for our next meeting.

Before I went to sleep, I thought about how our first French club meeting had gone much better than I expected. I liked the fact that the club was bigger than just me and Joni. It seemed to make it more official. Sean was definitely *mystérieux,* and kind of cute, although I'm not interested in that kind of thing right now. I need to focus on getting to France.

Samedi, 7 Avril

I went to the Brooklyn Botanic Garden with my *grand-mère.* This is one of the special things we do together. We have other special things we do: go to old movies (*Stage Door, The Women, Breakfast at Tiffany's*), thrift stores, and the Wonder Wheel at Coney Island. On special occasions, we go shopping at Bergdorf's and have tea in this really pretty round room at the Waldorf-Astoria. My *grand-mère* used to be a dressmaker, so she knows all about clothes. She made the dresses for her purple hat club and the other members all think she's a genius.

When we got to the benches next to the rose garden, she gave me a present, a red dress from her collection. Her collection is a steamer trunk in her bedroom that has all these really cool old clothes. And they fit me, unlike my mother's hand-me-downs, which are always tight. This red dress was made of delicious nubbly wool, knee-length and with a high collar and an adorable little matching jacket. I love it. I held the dress up in front of me so she could see what it would look like on.

"This is perfect, *Grand-mère.* Very Chanel. You must have looked hot in it."

"I had my moments, Lotus. You wouldn't think it to look at me now, but when I met your grandfather, I had quite the figure. I remember I had this blue silk shantung dress, with all these tiny pearl buttons, and a matching pillbox hat—it was so elegant. We used to go dancing on the weekends. Your grandfather loved to dance: the waltz, the rumba, the cha-cha."

My *grand-mère* started doing a few steps, back and forth, singing, "One, two, cha-cha-cha."

She grabbed my hand and we spun around the empty rose garden, my *grand-mère*, the red dress, and me. After a few spins, she was breathing hard and had to sit down.

While my *grand-mère* caught her breath, I held the dress up in front of me again and modeled it down a make-believe runway in front of her, swishing from side to side. "I could be in the purple hat club with this," I said, sticking one hip out like a model.

"No, it's purple dresses and red hats, Lotus. And that reminds me," she said, folding the dress neatly and then giving it back to me, "I've signed you up for the Race for the Cure."

"The what?"

"Race for the Cure. It's the breast cancer walk. It'll be fun. My ladies are all doing it, but I wanted you to come too."

"Okay, send me an e-mail so I'll know when it is."

My *grand-mère* loves e-mail. Almost every day, she sends me jokes, funny pictures, bloopers, thoughts of the day. She had breast cancer a few years ago, but she's fine now. I'm not dying to spend a day hanging around with the red hat ladies, but if she wants me to go, I guess I'll go.

"Is Mom going?"

She shook her head. "Your mother's very busy, and she's got a lot of events."

My mom works in development for a local arts organization, which means she spends a lot of time asking people for money and arguing with the board of directors. When my grandmother and my mother are together, they always fight, so why was she defending her now?

"Yeah, I guess."

"Your father . . ." She started to say something but stopped.

"He's working on a new play," I told her. "It's going to be really good. *Magnifique*."

She blew her nose into her handkerchief. "I sincerely hope so, Lotus. But in the meantime, you should give your mother a hand, help her out."

"Are you kidding? That's all I do; it's like I'm an indentured servant! My brother does *rien*."

My *grand-mère* patted me on the head like a puppy. "You're a good girl, Lotus."

We walked down to the rectangular reflecting pool, where, in the spring, they have lily pads. Nothing was really blooming yet, but I've always liked this time of year, when the garden isn't one thing or the other.

"So, how are things, my little latke? How is life?"

"*Pas mal*, not bad. I have a new job and I started a French club."

"That's wonderful, Lotus. Maybe you'll be one of those UN translators."

My *grand-mère* is the only family member who appreciates my love of all things Gallic. She adores all things Chanel. For my birthday last year, she gave me Allure, the "younger" Chanel fragrance. I spritz it on my neck every day, although my mother says it aggravates her allergies and is full of chemicals.

"And boys, my little heartbreaker?"

"All quiet on the *garçon* front, I'm afraid." An image of Sean popped into my head, but I pushed it right out.

When I got home, I tried on my red dress and showed my mother.

"It's very nice," she said, fingering the fabric. "Very well made, but don't you think it's a little old for you, Lotus?"

"No. As Coco Chanel said, 'Fashion fades, only style remains the same.' "

"Hmmm." My mother walked around me slowly. "And, I'm not sure it's really flattering on you."

"What do you mean?"

"Here"—she pointed to my hips—"it just seems a little tight."

"No, Maman, that's the way it's supposed to be."

She lay down on the floor on her heating pad in a disapproving kind of way.

"Grandma said she wore the dress to a party and she was the belle of the ball," I insisted.

"Yes, but back then, women were . . . they were more voluptuous."

"Well, I think it looks good. *Fantastique*. Let's see what Dad says."

"He's at his playwriting workshop. Listen, could you call Tofu Palace and order some dinner?" Instantly, my mother's tone went from disapproving to "Poor me, my back hurts, I'm just going to lie here while you do everything."

"And could you reheat this?" She held up her smelly herbal heating pad.

I reached down and grabbed the heating pad. "I hate Tofu Palace. I'm going to make an omelette with fines herbes."

"I really think you should watch it on the eggs, Lotus, and the cheese." My mother made a face. "Cholesterol is a killer, and you know that heart disease runs in our family."

"I read in *Yoga Journal* that if you feel good about your food while you're eating it, it's good for you."

"Okay, fine. I'm too tired to argue about it. Just order for me and your brother. There's money on the counter."

"Okay, okay, I'm on it."

I called Tofu Palace and ordered brown rice and tofu for my mother, sesame noodles and kung pao chicken for my brother, and some shrimp toast for me in case I needed a snack later. For dinner, we ate apart and had no family bonding, which was fine because I was able to read. My mother continued to lie on the floor and then talked on the phone with her friend Nanette and my brother took his food up to his room.

I ate my omelette, which kind of stuck to the pan and had perhaps too much oregano, in the dining room, with a candle and a copy of *The Second Sex*, by Simone de Beauvoir. Like Simone, I will never marry and never have children. I will live a life of freedom, not one of oppression at the hands of some man.

Dimanche, 8 Avril

Raining today—I slept late.
Contemplated the meaninglessness of existence.
Had cappuccino with Papa.
Got ready to study.
Organized my closet.
Painted toenails red (made small nail-polish-remover stain on coffee table, covered it up with ugly ceramic pot).
Took a nap.

Then I made a list of the gazillion things I had to do, my *choses à faire:*

> *French homework, ennuyant (annoying)*
> *Remember to go to job after school on Monday*
> *Get more food for French diet (European butter, baguettes,*
> *   dark chocolate, leeks)*
> *English homework*
> *Math homework*
> *Chores—clean bathroom (yech)*
> *Become fluent in French*
> *Plan outfit for next French club meeting*

I wonder if Sean will continue coming to our meetings. I hope so. I considered telling my *grand-mère* about him, but then she'll think I'm in love with him, which I definitely am *not.* Joni, on the other hand, can't stop talking about Sean. She thinks he looks like a movie star, but then again, Joni has had very little experience of a sexual nature. I, however,

French-kissed a guy at that fitness retreat my mother made me go on last year. It was an interesting experience—the kiss, not the fitness retreat, which was awful. I also got felt up during a trust exercise at acting camp. The relationships didn't last—in fact, I never spoke to either guy again—but I think the experiences were still valuable.

Lundi, 9 Avril

Work—boring.
I got my check—yeah!
Opened up the envelope and thought there had been a huge mistake. They took out an enormous amount of money for things I never agreed to, like Medicare and Social Security. I asked Barbara if she could do anything about it, explained how I really needed all the money for France, but she said no, that I needed to put money into the system. She was wearing clogs today. I thought of telling her that heels would make her ankles look slimmer, but decided against it.
Merde.

Jeudi, 12 Avril

We had the second meeting of French club last night. I couldn't get the movie *Before Sunrise*, but I rented another classic French movie with one of my absolute idols, Catherine Deneuve. It's called *Repulsion*.
We decided to make authentic *croque-monsieurs* (toasted ham and Gruyère cheese sandwiches) in Joni's toaster oven, although she only had cheddar cheese and English muffins,

so they were not entirely authentic. Her parents were at some law association dinner, so we had the place to ourselves for a few hours. I wore the new/old red jacket from my grandmother and my Levi's straight-leg jeans, which seem to have shrunk a little in the wash. Joni was in her usual fleece vest and Lee jeans, but when I walked in, I immediately knew something was different about her, in a good way.

I examined her up close. "Oh my God, you're wearing lipstick, aren't you?"

Joni looked embarrassed. "Um yeah, well, lip gloss."

I never leave the house without eyeliner, powder, and mascara, but I had never seen Joni wear makeup before. I'm not a big fan of shiny lip gloss, but I tried to be supportive. "It looks good, Joni, really."

The last guy Joni was seriously obsessed with was that Olympic skater Anton Ohno, who was on *Dancing With the Stars*. We used to have to watch hours and hours of dancing and old footage of his speed skating, until I felt dizzy. For as long as I've known her, Joni has had crushes on unavailable guys. When we were little, she liked Justin Timberlake (not my type at all), and later, Nick from Jonas Brothers. At least now she's decided to like someone closer to home.

When Sean got there, he told Joni he liked her glasses and that he liked my red jacket. He was being very *charmant*. I called the meeting to order and took the minutes on a legal pad I had stolen from my mother. I wanted to take a vote on something, but couldn't think of anything.

Sean picked up the DVD. "*Repulsion*, cool!"

We were going to have the meeting all in French, but Joni hasn't learned French yet, and Sean and I didn't want to make her feel uncomfortable. We voted to have it in English.

The meeting went well. We ate the *croque-monsieurs* and talked about school and then watched the movie. We sat squished on the couch with Sean in the middle. Catherine Deneuve was really beautiful, but the movie was kind of creepy. Her sister left her alone in this apartment and then she slowly went insane, ironing a lot and seeing stuff crawling around on the walls. We took a vote to turn off the film in the middle because Joni and I were getting too freaked out and felt we were having nervous breakdowns. Sean voted to keep it on, but we had the majority. I decided to dye my hair blond like Catherine Deneuve.

Vendredi, 13 Avril

Emergency family meeting!

Somehow, due to misplaced paperwork, the parental units discovered that I am barely passing French class. So we had to have a family meeting, which involved everyone sitting around the dining table and me being lectured.

My mother, frowning: "Lotus, we are very disappointed in you."

My father, looking wounded: "Yes, Lotus, why couldn't you have come to us with this? Even if you couldn't talk to your mother, why couldn't you come to me?"

My mother, annoyed: "What do you mean, 'If you couldn't talk to your mother'? What is that? What are you implying? Lotus can talk to me about anything."

My brother, bored and kicking the table loudly: "Do I

really have to be here? What does all this remedial stuff possibly have to do with me?"

My father: "Adam, we're a family and we're going to work this out together."

Me: "Look, I don't see what the big deal is. I retook the test I almost failed and I've really been studying my verbs and stuff. *Je suis sûre.*"

My brother: "The big deal, Lotus, is that you won't get into any college with your lame grades. Do you want to work at that granola bar your entire life?"

Me: "Do you mean the Wellness Center? No, but . . ."

My mother, to Adam: "There's no need to be cruel. Lotus, we're worried about you."

Me: "I'm fine." But honestly, I felt like a delinquent—like I should run out and get a tattoo or a piercing or something.

My father: "Honey, do you want us to get you some tutoring?"

My mother: "Don't you think you should check with me before suggesting something that might be very expensive, Daniel? But yes, Lotus, do you think that would help?"

Me: "I don't know. I guess. No."

My father: "Maybe this job is too much for you?"

My mother, glaring at my father: "You *would* think that."

My father: "Now who's being cruel?"

My brother: "Can I go now?"

My mother: "Well, okay, but I want you to be supportive of your sister in this."

My brother, calling down from the top of the stairs: "Mom, I can't help her, I took Latin, remember?"

After the meeting was over, I glanced at the newspaper that was lying on the table. It was almost Easter and apparently they've discovered that Judas wasn't such a bad guy after all. *Quelle surprise*. It was also Passover, which meant that we would soon be going over to my aunt Sarah's to listen to folk songs, eat enormous quantities of brisket, and read from a feminist Haggadah (a Haggadah is like the operating manual to the Passover seder, which tells you what to do when, and why you're doing it).

We have next week off from school for the holidays, but I'm not going to be enjoying it because I will be spending the whole time slaving at the Wellness Center and trying to study so I won't flunk out of school and end up working at Key Food, not that there is anything wrong with that, as my mother would say, although she would never actually do it herself.

At dinner (take-out Thai), I tried to bring up the fact that we are totally nonreligious Jews, so I didn't think I should have to go to any brainwashing religious ceremony. My father told me that we were going because it's the right thing to do. I quote: "Lotus, family is very important. We may not agree with all the doctrine, but the tradition is important." Then Adam started singing the song "Tradition" from *Fiddler on the Roof*.

Personally, I hate tradition and ritual. It's so last week. I am dedicated to living in the moment. I tried to get the parental units to let me go to Easter at Joni's in the interest of equal religious time and exploring other cultures (and perhaps getting an Easter basket filled with chocolate and Peeps), but that was a no-go.

Samedi, 14 Avril

Exhausted by my life—had to rest for most of the day.

Dimanche, 15 Avril

My *grand-mère* and I went to the William Wegman exhibit at the Brooklyn Museum. It was *très intéressant* and it wasn't just pictures of dogs. Wegman did a lot of other cool artwork when he was young, like those where he took found objects and pasted them on paintings. The exhibit was called Funney/Strange and it was both. Some people think that his photos of dogs are bizarre and exploitative, but I think he's an existentialist, like me, and appreciates the absurdity of life.

Afterward, my *grand-mère* dragged me to a Jewish mosaic tile exhibit from antiquity, which I thought would be *très* boring but was actually kind of cool, if you just ignored all the religious symbology and admired the patterns for their beauty. After going to the museum, I decided to become an artist. I tried to pose *Pierre le chien* in my skirt with the cherries, but he just slid right out of it. I watched two episodes of *Dog Whisperer* so I could learn how to be the pack leader, but Cesar Millan's techniques had no effect on Pierre. Perhaps this is because of his new French name and French attitude.

Lundi, 16 Avril

I cleaned my closets today and found a cute paisley shirt that I had forgotten about.

Thought about studying.

Mardi, 17 Avril

I tried to make homemade yogurt on the stove, but it ended up splattering all over the kitchen. Luckily, *Pierre le chien* likes yogurt. I attempted to take artistic pictures of Pierre with yogurt on his face, but he refused to look moody and started licking the camera. Considered making carrot soup, but we don't have a food mill or any of the other important cooking implements of a French kitchen.

Mercredi, 18 Avril

I worked at the Wellness Center all day. Spoke with many cranky pregnant women with cranky allergic children. I'm exhausted. Not sure I could cope with a full-time job. How do people do it? Ate too much at lunch (ham and Brie on baguette, *salade*, chocolate bar) and fell asleep (only for a moment) at the reception desk until Sheila started coughing loudly. It's not my fault they won't let me drink Starbucks coffee. How are you supposed to stay awake drinking herbal tea? I told Barbara how caffeine prevents Alzheimer's, but she said I was a little too young to worry about Alzheimer's.

Jeudi, 19 Avril

Passover was the usual. Relatives kissing me on the cheek and saying how "healthy" I look. Everyone fawned over Adam because of his chess games. No hors d'oeuvres except carrot sticks and tasteless olives, bad wine (kosher?), carbs (potato kugel), more carbs (barley), even more carbs (matzo balls the size of my head). Then, a boring reading from a badly Xeroxed Haggadah.

Pharaoh
Egypt
Moses
Blah blah blah, Dayenu, blah blah blah

Rugelach (ick)

Here's a question: Just because they had to eat unleavened bread, why do we have to suffer?

Vendredi, 20 Avril

I have gotten nothing done all week, so today I am going to spend the entire day studying, only stopping for short espresso breaks. First, I tried to write a descriptive passage for Ms. G.

Park Slope
Strollers, strollers, and more strollers.
Obnoxious bikers, organic food, trees.

That's all I can think of for now.

Next, math. I did boring problems for an hour, but then needed a break desperately, so I called Joni and told her to meet me at the F train in a half hour with her mother's

Bloomingdale's card and an open mind. I was technically grounded for getting a D on my French test, but everyone seemed to be out (my father and Adam at some chess tournament, my mother at a conference), so what was the harm?

I decided to use very scientific principles from *What Not to Wear* (both the American and the British versions) to get Joni out of her sweatshirts and mom-style Lee jeans. These principles are very strict. First, no tapered pants and no capris. No shapeless, ill-fitting clothes and *absolument* no overalls! Third and most important, a properly fitting bra, but not a sports bra, *quelle horreur!*

Shopping was exhausting. I used to think being a personal shopper would be an easy job, but *mon Dieu*, was I wrong! We were waiting outside a dressing room in the designer dress section, where every high school senior and her overly protective mother were shopping for the ugliest prom dresses in the universe. Here's one good thing about my mom: She would never encourage me to go to my prom, even though it's years away. She has some horrible memory from hers involving corsages and disco and Boone's Farm apple wine. Joni and I gradually slid down the puke-colored walls of the dressing room until we were sitting cross-legged on the dusty floor with all of the clothes I had picked out piled around us. The dressing-room nazi told us we couldn't sit there, so we stood up again.

"This is absurd," I said. "What are those people doing in there, giving birth?"

There were ten individual dressing rooms, but no one had emerged in twenty minutes. Finally, an annoying skinny girl wearing a dull green cotton dress with ugly flower appliqués came out of a room. She couldn't have found a dress that looked worse on her if she had spent all day trying. It was strapless and frilly, and the color made her look like she had the bird flu. Annoying Girl twirled around, showing the dress to her corporate boyfriend, who was talking on a cell phone and ignoring her. I rolled my eyes at Joni, who was now leaning on a wall, trying to keep upright under the weight of all the clothes I had selected for her to try on.

"*Cette robe est ridicule,*" I said to Joni.

"If you're saying that dress is ugly, I agree."

I looked over at the nine other dressing-room doors, which remained closed. When the saleslady left to get more dresses for Annoying Girl, I put on my most official-sounding voice and announced:

"Please vacate the dressing rooms for routine maintenance. There will be men coming any minute!"

One lady actually listened to me and left her dressing room. Joni and I grabbed her room and collapsed on the floor, laughing. Unfortunately, Joni hated everything she tried on. It was all "too tight," "too low-cut," "too slutty" for her. As she tried on a stretchy blue dress (which looked great), she asked me what I thought about Sean.

"Well, I suppose he isn't as completely shallow as some of the other high school males."

"He's kind of cute, right?" She tugged at the dress's hem, trying to make it longer.

"I suppose he does have style," I said grudgingly. "And he has those sleepy eyes."

"Did you hear about his parents?" asked Joni, taking off the dress and putting on a pair of jeans.

"No, I mean, he told me they were divorced. . . ."

"Well, my mom talked to Daria's mom, who met Sean's stepmother at Bikram yoga, and she told her that Sean's real mother just left one day. Went off with her dermatologist and now they live in Switzerland."

"You're kidding! And what about the stepmom? What did Daria's mom say about her?"

Joni took off the jeans, which were too big. "She just said she's obsessed with working out—apparently she does Bikram, like, six times a week."

"Isn't that all gross and sweaty?"

"Yeah, and the guys just wear these little shorts, so some-times their—"

"Ewww. Stop, Joni, please."

Joni laughed. "Okay."

I put the blue dress back on its hanger. "I wonder if he ever gets to see his mother?"

"Probably not too often."

"Poor Sean. Maybe that's why he seems so lonerish."

"Lotus, you're not, you know, interested in him, are you?"

"You know he's way too young for me, but he does have a certain *je ne sais quoi*."

I finally convinced Joni to buy some jeans that actually fit her and a cute black T-shirt with a deep V-neck. We also got her a pretty black bra and I got a very attractive lacy red number, because all French women have incredible, sexy underwear. Joni treated me to the bra and lunch on her mother's credit card because I was working so hard as her stylist.

Dimanche, 22 Avril

I woke up late, ate two croissants, and had a café au lait. Read a few pages of *Nausea*, by Jean-Paul Sartre, and started to feel a little nauseated myself. I think it was because I totally related to the way J.P. felt about everything. Like how he looked at something and couldn't even remember what it is or why it is. That's how I feel. I mean, what's the point? I'll never have enough money to go to France. I'll never fall in love. It's just one endless day after the other.

I knocked on my father's study door.

"Enter at your own risk," he boomed.

"Hey, Dad, how's it going?"

"If writing one page every four hours and then realizing it's crap is the criteria, then I'm doing fantastically."

"That sucks, Dad, but listen, this is important. I've been doing a lot of thinking and I've decided life is meaningless."

He shook my hand and patted me on the back. Hard. "Congratulations, Lotus. Many great philosophers have spent their whole lives studying and ruminating before coming to that very same conclusion."

"So, now what do I do?"

"Aye, that's the rub."

"Thanks, Dad, that was real helpful." I left him staring at a blank computer screen.

I went over to Joni's to study. She was wearing her same old boring sweatshirt and jeans.

"Hey, Joni, why aren't you wearing your new jeans? The ones I grabbed from that girl before she took the last one in your size. They looked really good on you."

She shrugged.

"I mean, it's not like you're Mormon or something and have to wear baggy, shapeless clothes so you won't drive guys insane with lust."

Joni's mom walked in as I said that. She smiled. "No, Lotus, you're right: We're not Mormons, we're Protestants."

"Hi, Mrs. Davis." Joni's mom was wearing low-rise black pants and a T-shirt that looked very casual yet very expensive.

"See, Joni, even your mother agrees that you have no valid reason not to wear the jeans and the cute shirt you bought."

Joni pushed her hair behind her ears. "I will, I will, stop bugging me."

"She has such an adorable figure, doesn't she?" said Joni's mom, patting Joni on the butt.

Joni moved away from her mother. "Mom, stop, you're embarrassing me."

I nodded, looking at Joni's mom. "I know, and she can eat anything without gaining a pound."

"Would you guys stop talking about me like I'm not here," complained Joni.

"What you need, Joni, is to develop an individual style, like me." (I was wearing a T-shirt with a picture of *la Tour Eiffel*, black pedal pushers—which are totally different than capris—flats, and a red scarf tied jauntily around my neck.) "You need a signature look so you'll make an impression."

Joni's mom looked at me and then looked at Joni. "Yes, Joni. Not that you want to look exactly like Lotus, but you could be a little more—"

"*Féminine, individuelle*," I suggested.

Joni's mom nodded. "Yes."

Joni rolled her eyes. "I like my clothes just the way they are. Mom, please leave. And Lotus, come on, we really need to study!"

"*D'accord.*"

"I'll leave you girls to it, then." Joni's mother sighed and went downstairs.

Joni flopped on her bed. "Lotus, I swear, if you ever gang up with my mother again . . ."

"Sorry, sorry, but you do have a great figure."

Joni folded her arms over her chest. "I don't know what you're talking about. I'm totally flat-chested and I don't have a butt and my knees are all knobby and disgusting."

"You're insane. That's what you are. Insane."

We studied for a while. I concentrated on memorizing French phrases that will come in handy when I am living in France.

Ce vin sent le bouchon: This wine is corked.

Si beau qu'il fasse, je ne peux pas sortir: No matter how nice the weather is, I can't go out.

Si gentil que tu sois, je ne t'aime pas: However kind you are, I don't love you.

Then we brainstormed about our next French club meeting. I made a list of possible activities.

Idées:

Music: Edith Piaf, Jacques Brel, Les Sans Culottes (they have a song called "Tout Va Bien").

Movie: The French Connection, French Kiss, The French Lieutenant's Woman.

French conversation: Joni's French is still not up to par, although she has learned some curse words.

Food: I'm thinking fondue.

"Do you think Sean'll come to the next meeting?" asked Joni, doodling in her notebook.

"He'd better. We should find out his schedule, though." I made a note in my notebook, then I looked at Joni, who looked so eager, like *Pierre le chien* when he really wants to go for a walk.

"Hey, why don't you call him and find out when he's free?" I suggested, and Joni nodded, acting like it wasn't a big deal.

As I was leaving, Joni's mom grabbed my arm.

"Lotus, I just wanted to let you know that when you get home, you need to ask your mom to buy a safety kit from the Red Cross. For the next tsunami. I just watched a BBC documentary. This is serious. It could wipe out the entire East Coast and you'll have to get twelve miles inland." She led me over to a closet near the front door. It was filled with row after row of bottled water and Pom.

"So, Lotus, remember, just go on Google and type 'mega-tsunami.' "

"Okay, Mrs. Davis. I'll do that."

I could see Joni rolling her eyes behind her mother's back.

"Call me Julia."

"Okay, Julia. Ciao, Joni. Ciao, Julia."

It was my father's night to make dinner and we had salmon with salad and couscous, although I wasn't sure he had actually cooked anything because I saw some take-out containers in the kitchen.

Over dinner, I told *ma famille* there was going to be a mega-tsunami and Joni's mom, Julia, said we needed to buy supplies. My mother shook her head. "Julia says, Julia says. Lotus, that woman's grip on reality is not too tight. That's the kind of paranoid insular thinking that happens when you don't have a real job—you have too much time to obsess over nonsense."

"Oh, and we also need to get twelve miles inland," I added.

"That's so lame," said Adam. "Even if this cataclysmic event did happen, which is only slightly statistically proba-ble in the next hundred years, you wouldn't be able to get out. Think about it, Lotus. Millions of people trying to get out of Brooklyn at the same time. Limited points of egress. Driving or walking, you'd be toast."

"Thanks, Adam, you're such a comfort." I punched him lightly in the arm.

"Ow."

"I hardly touched you, you baby."

My mother turned to me. "Lotus, remember that word, *egress*. That's a good SAT word. It means 'exit.' "

"Maybe the earth is meant to be destroyed," said my fa-ther, taking a sip of wine.

"Just ignore Julia, Lotus. Daniel, this is organic salmon, right?" asked my mother, her fork poised over her plate.

My father sounded annoyed. "It's whatever they had at the fish store. Anyway, Suki, if I followed every ridiculous food rule you have, we'd starve."

"Daniel, are you aware that mercury and PCBs can affect cognitive development in children?"

"Well, given that Adam just won his third chess tournament, I think you can relax."

My mother looked over at me and sighed.

I pushed my salmon back and forth with my fork. "Hey, don't look at me—I don't even like salmon; I just pretend to eat it."

My father waved his glass at my mother. "Lotus's cognitive functions are fine, Suki. She just has some trouble focusing because she's a creative person."

"I guess you would know," said my mother, pushing her salmon carefully to the side of her plate as if it were radioactive.

After dinner, I went to my room. I was unable to do my English homework, since all I could think about was a giant wave of water hitting our brownstone and how my life had no meaning and how unprepared I was.

I went online and found out what I needed to assemble my own disaster kit on the Red Cross Web site.

Assemble a Disaster Supplies Kit, Including the Following Items:

First-aid kit and essential medications.
Canned food and can opener.
At least three gallons of water per person.
Protective clothing, rainwear, and bedding or sleeping bags.

Battery-powered radio, flashlight, and extra batteries.
Special items for infants, elderly, or disabled family members.
Written instructions on how to turn off electricity, gas, and water
if authorities advise you to do so.
(Remember, you'll need a professional to turn them back on.)

I left a copy of the list under my parents' door, and then I wrote a note to Ms. G explaining about Joni's mom and the safety kit and how hard it was to do homework when the world might be coming to an end.

Lundi, 23 Avril

School was too boring to describe. Joni wore her new jeans, although I could tell she felt really self-conscious. I wore a yellow Pucci-esque dress I got at a thrift store and my white go-go boots. Mr. Higgleston said I looked classy, although a few of the so-called popular girls were whispering about me when I went by their lockers. I don't care what they say. I enjoy attention, whether it's positive or negative. They're just jealous, anyway, because they are all Abercrombie & Fitch clones and have no sense of personal style. They probably don't even know who Pucci is.

After school, I went to the Wellness Center. It was pretty slow, so I read magazines and tried to do my homework. Whenever I picked up a magazine, I heard Sheila making weird noises behind me—yowns and sowns (sigh plus groan).

Finally, I turned around and asked her if she was sleep deprived, and mentioned that I had read in *Natural Health* magazine that your bedroom should be an oasis of calm: soft lights, no TV (she's addicted to television, especially *Deal or No Deal* and *The Amazing Race*). That kept her quiet for a little while.

Mardi, 24 Avril

Got back my homework.

Lotus,

While I'm sure that your friend's mother is genuinely worried about disasters, you should realize that people have a tendency to project their inner anxieties onto external events. So, while I appreciate that modern life is uncertain, I don't think that Park Slope, Brooklyn, is under imminent danger this semester from a mega-tsunami, and therefore, I can't give you a permanent extension on your paper to prepare a safety kit. If you're concerned, a little extra water and a flashlight are probably always good ideas.
Ms. G

four

Assignment #4

Things That Give a Pathetic Impression

The voice of someone who blows his nose while he is speaking. The expression of a woman plucking her eyebrows.
—Sei Shōnagon

Things That Make Me Cringe

A fat person feeding their fat child ice cream (cruel). A thin person feeding their child tofu dogs (gross and cruel, I've tasted them).
—Lotus Lowenstein

Mercredi, 25 Avril

Today, I met with Ms. G about French club.

She was wearing boring black pants and a baggy black turtleneck.

"Ms. G, have you ever tried color near your face? I think it would make your eyes pop."

"Lotus, we're here to talk about you, and to be frank, I'm not sure I want my eyes to pop. It sounds kind of unpleasant."

"No," I tried to explain, "it just means that your eyes would look really blue. Trust me."

"I'll think about it, but in the meantime, Lotus, let's get back to your idea of a French club."

"If you insist."

Ms. G adjusted her glasses. "So, Lotus, what's the purpose of the club?"

"To soak up French culture, *bien sûr.*"

"Well, that's a good start, but I think we're going to need something more concrete. A goal, perhaps. An educational trip or a project. Something like that."

"Well, as you know, I am planning to go to France, but I always imagined myself going alone, *seule*, that is."

"France might be a little bit ambitious for the club, but it's definitely something you should do at some point. Have you thought of taking a year abroad when you're in college?"

"No offense, but I'm not sure traditional education has much to offer me."

Ms. G smiled. "I know it doesn't seem that meaningful now, but I promise you, you'll regret it if you don't go."

"*Je ne* plan on regretting *rien*, as Edith Piaf said."

"How about Montreal for the French club? That's a nice, manageable goal. Not too expensive, not too far. You could raise some money and perhaps we could get the administration to kick in some funds if there are educational activities."

"*Fantastique.*"

"You know that if the school kicks in funding, you will have to have an adult accompany you? Maybe one of your parents?"

"Why can't you come with us?"

"Well, I suppose I could, but usually a parent wants to be involved. Why don't you talk it over with the other members of the club and your parents."

"*Dac*—that's short for *d'accord*, which means 'okay.'"

"Okay, Lotus, thanks. So, keep notes at the meetings and let's have an update in a few weeks, okay?"

"*Oui*, but Ms. G, just remember this one thing, okay? Wear color with color."

After the meeting with Ms. G, I feel a little less meaningless, since she obviously is in desperate need of my help, but I am still totally an existentialist.

Jeudi, 26 Avril

Another English assignment to do a list of stuff, à la Sei Shōnagon. I was basing mine on the following section from *The Pillow Book:*

> *I cannot stand a woman who wears sleeves of unequal width.*
> —*Sei Shōnagon*

Apparently, fashions were as stupid in Sei's day as in mine. People are still wearing those weird tops with only one arm that make them look like amputees.

Assignment # 5
Things I Cannot Stand

T-shirts with ridiculous sayings. Here are two I saw today:
REHAB IS FOR QUITTERS
Picture of a piñata with I'D HIT THAT *beneath it*

Sudoku: Talk about religion being the opiate of the masses. Everyone is still totally addicted to these stupid puzzles. I've even seen kids in school doing them, as if we don't have enough mindless homework to do.

People who listen to your phone calls and then comment on them (yes, I'm talking about you, Sheila the bookkeeper).

People who don't take your advice and are still wearing their old boring clothes when you went out of your way to give them a makeover.
—Lotus Lowenstein

Vendredi, 27 Avril

Family movie night was recently reinstituted, after our inability last year to reach consensus on movie choice. This year, we each take turns choosing. I picked *Bee Season* because it had Juliette Binoche, but I'm not sure I liked it that much. In the movie, Richard Gere was looking *très vieux* (very old) and was into kabbalah (like Madonna) and his son was a Goody Two-shoes (like my brother, Adam) who played cello and the daughter was a spelling-bee genius. The mother was nice, but went around to other people's houses stealing pieces of glass and putting them into a storage unit and they never totally explained why she was doing it and the little girl lost the important spelling bee on the word *origami* (which she totally knew) because winning was too important to her father. Maybe it would have been better in *français*.

After the movie, my mother turned to my father and said, "See," as if it were his fault that Juliette Binoche was a klepto. He just shrugged and said that he was thinking of looking into mysticism and Adam was like, "Next time I get to pick the movie."

Samedi, 28 Avril

Sean called me this morning. He wanted to meet and discuss Jean-Paul Sartre, the *père* of existentialism. I took him to the Brooklyn Botanic Garden. My first thought was to call and tell Joni, but I didn't because I knew she'd want to come with us. I knew I was being a bad friend, but I really wanted to spend some time with Sean alone.

It was the Cherry Blossom Festival and there were masses of religious long-skirt people and tourists getting their pictures taken in family clumps. I know it's probably politically incorrect, but they were really annoying me. I mean, what's up with the long denim skirts, and enough with the cameras, people. I wondered what Sei Shōnagon would think about the Japanese Garden. I think she would have to be annoyed by all the tourists and their cameras too.

Sean and I sat down on the part of the grass where you're allowed to lie down, but not to eat or drink anything because it might attract rodents or destroy the grass. There was a woman guard who was walking back and forth staring at us to see if we were doing anything wrong. It was so nice, lying next to Sean, looking up at the sky. I don't know why, but I feel so comfortable with him. I had brought potato chips and we snuck them one at a time when the guard walked over to the other side and couldn't see us. One time when she walked by, I almost choked on a chip.

"She's such a fascist," whispered Sean in my ear.

"Yeah," I agreed, trying to remember the exact difference between Fascists and Nazis. I thought the Fascists were Italian and the Nazis were German, but it was kind of confusing. Sean never took off his leather jacket, even though it was *très* warm in the sun. I thought about what I had said to Joni about Sean being too young for me. It was true, but nevertheless, I felt so good, lying there next to him, knowing that his arm was only inches from mine. Probably just my raging teenage hormones.

We discussed Sartre. Sean knew an amazing lot about him, like that he was in prison for a while and that both he and Simone used to do amphetamines. I told him that they were never married but were buried in the same grave. When I mentioned that I was reading *La Nausée,* he pulled a copy out of his back pocket and read me a passage about how weird the guy felt picking up a fork. We agreed to call Jean-Paul Sartre J.P. from now on.

I couldn't believe how comfortable I felt lying next to a *garçon*. I liked the feel of his arm next to mine, and more than that, I feel like I could talk to him forever. Why do Joni and I have to like the same *garçon*? Maybe she just has a crush on him and it isn't real, like her feelings for that kid from the Jonas Brothers, who she now thinks is really shallow, especially after I told her he had dated Miley Cyrus.

What were the odds of me meeting a boy who was cute and as obsessed with existentialism as I was in Park Slope, Brooklyn? When he pulled *La Nausée* out of his back pocket, I couldn't believe it. It was so amazing and *romantique* that we'd both been reading the same book at the same time. I had read about *coup de foudre*, love at first sight, but I couldn't believe it was happening to *moi*.

Dimanche, 29 Avril

I went to the library. Crowded. My choice of seats was at a table with a weird guy who looked like Jesus or at a table with an old crazy guy who probably smelled and who was surrounded by piles of decaying papers. I decided to take my book out and read it in the park.

I sat under a tree and read a book about Montreal. Apparently, the *Montréaliens* are very big on *le jazz*. They have a whole festival devoted to *le jazz*. My dad listens to jazz, but I don't care for it because it makes my heart beat funny. I am sad that Montreal is not Paris, but *peut-être* it could be a trial run to see how I function in a French-speaking culture. It is the second-largest French-speaking city in the world, after all. I pictured Sean and me in a dark jazz club drinking Campari. Sean and I speaking French and drinking café au laits in tiny cafés. Sean and I walking around Montreal and having deep discussions about life and love and *l'existentialisme*.

Talked to Joni on the phone about Montreal. She was totally psyched. I thought about telling her that Sean and I had gone to the Botanic Garden, but decided against it. Joni is my best friend, and I've always told her everything, but this I couldn't tell her. I knew it was wrong, but I had never felt this way about anyone before. This could be *l'amour*, for real.

Mardi, 1 Mai

The third meeting of the French club was at Joni's house again, because her parents were at a fund-raiser for resistant staph infections. I couldn't wait to see Sean, and dressed extra carefully and put on two coats of mascara. I made fondue with my mother's old orange Le Creuset fondue set. When my mother dug it out from the back of the pantry, she started reminiscing about how she and *mon père* used to have these crazy parties where they danced and made fondue before she found out she was lactose intolerant.

Sean brought Gauloises cigarettes and a CD of a singer named Keren Ann who sings in French sometimes. I liked a song called "Dimanche en Hiver," which means "Sunday in

Winter," although in reality, it was Tuesday in the spring. Sean and I attempted to smoke by Joni's pool, but Joni kept getting paranoid about her parents finding out and spent most of the time waving the smoke away and DustBustering stray ashes. When Sean leaned in to light my Gauloises, I felt incredibly close to him. I did not inhale, but I fear I may have become addicted nevertheless, because even now I crave the feeling of having a cigarette in my hand. Joni wore her new V-neck shirt and extra lipstick (finally) and sat next to Sean at any opportunity. I wore a very narrow pencil skirt, which made it almost impossible to sit down at all. I was also wearing Power Panties, which my mother had bought me. They are supposed to keep your bulges in check, but they are so tight that you feel kind of faint (or maybe it was the cigarettes). I was a little nervous that Sean was going to tell Joni that we had hung out the other day, but he acted as if nothing had happened, probably for Joni's sake. She was talking to him so much, I barely had a chance to say anything.

The fondue was delicious except for the burnt parts, which stuck to the bottom of the pan and were incredibly *difficile* to wash out, so I just let the pot soak and told Joni I'd pick it up later.

We discussed Montreal, but no one had a good idea about how to raise the money. Joni suggested I ask my mom because that's what she does—raise money—although I couldn't help but think if she's so good at it, how come we never have any. We did have an official vote about going to Montreal. Everyone voted *oui*.

I was hoping to walk home with Sean, but he left first, and I stayed to help Joni clean up all evidence of smoking.

Mercredi, 2 Mai

My mom came into the Wellness Center yesterday, all cheerful. She gave me a big hug and kiss, which was kind of weird. I had to lean way over the desk to reach her, which was uncomfortable. "My favorite daughter," she said, patting me on the cheeks. "How was the fondue, darling?"

"It was bonne. Maman, you are not yourself, are you on *la drogue?*" I asked, but she just laughed.

Sheila popped up and told my mother how nice it was to have a young person around (meaning *moi*) and I felt nauseated. Then the new acupuncturist came out and led Maman away to be punctured by tiny needles. He was young, Italian, and cute. I wondered if French women got acupuncture. After she disappeared into the treatment room, I went back to entering boring patient records into a database that was probably used in prehistoric times. When my mom came out, she looked ten years younger. She told Sheila, "That man is an absolute magician. My back is in heaven."

After my mother left, Sheila kept hovering over me all afternoon, telling me how great my mother was. She probably thinks we're best friends now because we had a nanosecond of conversation. She offered to show me her Chico's catalog and give me Crock-Pot recipes. I told her I only liked to cook with fresh ingredients and not leave them to fester for ten hours and that I bought all my clothes at very exclusive consignment shops, not generic catalog stores. Then she starting telling me I was entering the patient records all wrong. *Impossible*. I couldn't see what she was talking about, because she had placed her entire body between me and my computer screen. She was muttering about subcategories and section codes and ID numbers and that we were going to have to redo everything.

I suggested that perhaps she didn't explain it to me correctly in the first place. She snorted loudly and continued to lecture me about how I knew nothing and had done it all wrong. Finally, when I couldn't take being in such close proximity to her breath, which smelled faintly of onions, I told her I had an urgent appointment and had to leave.

I went home and lay down with a cool compress over my eyes until Adam banged on my door and said Joni was here. Joni was *très* upset because her mother had written to the school to complain that we have no evacuation plan in case of a major disaster like a tsunami or bird flu. Joni was beyond embarrassed. I told her not to worry, that lots of people were freaked out about disasters. To calm her down, we watched old episodes of *America's Next Top Model*. My favorite wannabe model was Shandi, a gawky blonde from Cycle 2 who photographed very well. She was the most original, but didn't win. *Quelle surprise*.

Vendredi, 4 Mai

I invited Sean over to look at my Simone de Beavoir books. I tried to sneak him upstairs, but my mom came out from the kitchen and was all *Lotus darling, who is your young man*, like we were in an ancient play or something. He acted along and kissed her hand and she practically melted into the floor. Then she asked if he wanted to stay for dinner, which was not what I had in mind, but he said yes, he'd love to, before I could say anything. I told him it would probably be Thai takeout, but it turned out my mother had actually cooked, which she practically never does. She made some kind of tofu thing, which was okay if you told yourself it was goat cheese, not tofu, and that bland was interesting. Sean said it was *délicieux*.

Over dinner, my whole family fell in love with Sean. My father found out that Sean was interested in theater and offered to lend him his first edition of *An Actor Prepares*, by Stanislavski, and my mother kept getting up to fetch him more salad and Fizzy Lizzy sodas. Then he talked about chess with Adam and my family fell further under his spell and I ate two pieces of Junior's strawberry cheesecake.

After dinner, we watched a movie, *The Squid and the Whale*, which takes place in Brooklyn. It was pretty good, but I found it hard to pay attention with Sean there. Afterward, my mother said the mother character was really a famous movie reviewer named Georgia from the *Village Voice*, not a novelist, and my father said he had once met the real father, the writer Jonathan Baumbach, and that he was a depressive. "Probably more so now," said my mother, "after seeing the movie." Then my mother made me and my brother promise that we would never write about our family, but I crossed my fingers, so it doesn't count.

By then it was late, so Sean left without us getting any time alone, although he said he had a great time, and Adam and I had to clean up the kitchen. I asked Adam what he thought of Sean and he asked me if we had done it yet. I told him he was a pig. I then reminded him of how he used to play with dolls and he threw a dish towel at me and then we had a minor food fight involving tofu and broccoli. It was kind of like old times, when we used to hang out together and fake wrestle, before he became obsessed with chess.

Later, my mom and dad both made a point of telling me how great Sean was, as if I had finally accomplished something, and as I was going upstairs to bed, my mom said, "But don't get your hopes up, Lotus. Boys like Sean like to play the field."

Samedi, 5 Mai

I went to work, then saw my *grand-mère* for a shopping trip at a new thrift store, where I bought a cool sundress with little blue sailboats on it.

Dimanche, 6 Mai

Thought about Sean and how my family wants to adopt him now. I don't know why I'm surprised, it's been happening my whole life. When I was little, I'd bring a friend over to play Barbies. Then, I'd come home a few days later and my friend would be having cookies with Adam and my mom, and I would be the one left out.

Lundi, 7 Mai

Joni called and told me that she and Sean had gone to the Chocolate Room yesterday. They only serve desserts there and I've been dying to go. Fine. Great. I am not *jalouse*, because, like Simone de Beauvoir, I don't believe you can own another person. Of course, Simone was also into three-somes and lesbian affairs, which is definitely not my thing. Joni went on and on about how they had such a great time and how Sean was telling her all this stuff about existential-ism and she's thinking about reading some J.P. (I can't be-lieve he told her our special nickname for Sartre). After a while, I got sick of Joni talking about Sean and I told her that I had a migraine and had to go lie down.

I went and talked to my dad, who was working on an ad for *Backstage Magazine*. I was going to ask his advice, but he was too busy trying to write his ad for non-Equity actors, whatever they are. He told me that he was also going to apply for a playwriting grant, and he asked me to help him with the auditions. I said I would if I could get one of those director's chairs with my name on it.

I tried to study, but couldn't concentrate because I kept thinking about Sean and Joni discussing J.P. and eating chocolate fondue. I went into the kitchen to attempt yet again the *vrai* yogurt recipe from *French Women Don't Get Fat*, but the yogurt came out with the consistency and taste of paste. I was beginning to think there was something wrong with the recipe, because I followed it religiously, ex-cept I didn't have a thermometer to know when it reached one hundred ten degrees and I didn't have a jar, just a plastic container. I did everything else perfectly, though. The good news is that *Pierre le chien's* coat is extra glossy from all the French yogurt I've been feeding him. By the time I finished cleaning up the yogurt, I decided to tell Joni that Sean had come over for dinner. We're best friends, so we shouldn't have secrets, and if Sean and I are going to be seeing a lot of each other, she'll have to get used to it. If she's my true friend, she'll understand that *l'amour* cannot be denied.

This is how it went:

Me: "Hey, I forgot to tell you that Sean came over to my house for dinner the other night."

Joni (sounding hurt): "I can't believe you didn't call me."

Me: "I thought you were busy that night. Don't you have physics club on Fridays?"

Joni: "Lotus, I don't even take physics yet—that's senior year."

Me: "Oops. Hey, it's not like you called when you guys had your rendezvous at the Chocolate Room."

Joni: "That is so not true. We did call, on my cell. Didn't Adam tell you? You were at work. If you'd get a cell phone, you wouldn't have to miss things."

Me: "Well, you know how my parents feel about cell phones. They're practically Luddites, and they're cheap, too. I'm surprised your mom lets you have one because of all the health risks."

Joni: "She thinks natural disasters trump medical things. Anyway, from now on, promise you'll call if you and Sean are going to hang out. I don't want to miss anything."

Me (fingers crossed): "I'll definitely try to remember."

Assignment #6
Suprising and Distressing Things

A carriage overturns. One would have imagined that such a solid, bulky object would remain forever on its wheels. It all seems like a dream—astonishing and senseless.
—Sei Shōnagon

When it's raining really hard, with masses of thunder and streaks of lightning, and you start to think that your umbrella may be a lightning rod, and yet, you can't let go of it. ·

Zombie movies. Woke up in the middle of the night after seeing Resident Evil, afraid to move because my family might all have turned into flesh-eating zombies. In the morning, luckily, they turned out to be human.

Tsunami that is going to destroy the entire East Coast. The other night Adam and I watched this movie called Deep Impact where only certain people were going to get to live in this underground cave after the tsunami hit and New York was pretty much destroyed and even the Statue of Liberty toppled over. What really got to me was this scene where Téa Leoni and her father just stand there hugging on the beach she went to as a child, while this giant wave crashes into them. What would that be like, just standing there knowing that you are going to die? When I was little, I used to lie in bed and give myself a

panic attack trying to imagine death, what it would feel like, what it would be like to have no more me. That's why I won't go see that Al Gore movie about global warming and sometimes I wish I were a catholique and knew there was going to be an afterlife.
—*Lotus Lowenstein*

Dear Lotus,

I was a little concerned about you after reading your latest assignment. If you ever need to talk, feel free to set up an appointment. Are you experiencing any special stress at home? I don't know if it will make you feel any better, but as far as the tsunami is concerned, the odds of dying from one are around 1 in 500,000, so I want you to stop worrying and perhaps institute a moratorium on disaster and zombie movies. And lastly, Lotus, for your next Pillow Book assignment, I want you to pick something positive.

Ms. G

Mardi, 8 Mai

My father has set up a date to have auditions for his play. It's *très* exciting. He's gotten hundreds of headshots in the mail and even my mother seems slightly impressed. I'm thinking of getting my own headshot taken. I suggested to *mon père* that he should put some J.P. quotes into his play and he said he'd think about it. I told him my favorite: *She believed in nothing; only her skepticism kept her from being an atheist.* That's so me.

Mercredi, 9 Mai

"Hell is other people," I pronounced at breakfast, such as it was (cardboard cereal and soy milk).

"Wasn't that Dorothy Parker who said that?" asked my mother.

"No, it was J.P., I mean, Sartre. And why can't we have real milk?"

"Soy is good for you, Lotus. I care about your health. Not like my mother, who fed us chicken fat and fried salami."

"You're right, Lotus," said my father, responding in his absentminded-professor way. "Dorothy Parker was 'Men don't make passes at girls who wear glasses.' " He smiled at my mother, who was wearing her reading glasses and doing the *New York Times* crossword puzzle.

"Are you trying to tell me something, Daniel?" asked my mother, pulling off her glasses.

"Don't get me all worked up, Suki," my father said sarcastically, squeezing my mother's shoulders as he walked past to get more coffee.

"Wasn't Dorothy Parker a big alcoholic?" interjected Adam, and then my father started telling us some boring stuff about a round table and an Algonquin and then they segued into a discussion of the Iraq War blah blah oil blah blah the administration blah blah people I never heard of blah blah blah.

Jeudi, 10 Mai (Audition Night!)

When all the actors sauntered in, I took their headshots, wrote their names down on a yellow legal pad, gave them the script to look over, and called their names when my father was ready for them. I wore my blue peplum suit that makes me look like a movie star. For a moment I toyed with the idea of becoming an actress, but the thought of playing anyone other than *moi* seems kind of boring. Some of the actors were cute, but some of them were *très* annoying, asking for glasses of water and clearing their throats very loudly and making weird *baa baa baa* noises, like demented sheep.

I called Sean so he could come over and see their weirdness. This one guy shook all over like a dog before he auditioned. Sean confided in me that he would like to be an actor too. I said he could be the modern-day James Dean, without the dying-young part. Joni called in the midst of the auditions and asked what I was doing, so I had to invite her over too. I told her I had been about to call, but my mother had been on a conference call.

Joni arrived wearing a pink T-shirt that she had gotten at the American Apparel on Flatbush Avenue. She told us that they made all their clothes in the United States, so she wasn't wearing sweatshop-labor clothes. I told her I thought that was great, but I didn't really understand why it was so great—I mean it's not like American Apparel was going to go down to the Third World and get those sweatshop people a different job somewhere else.

Sean sat *très* close to Joni as we did mock readings from the scripts. They were sharing a script, but I didn't see why they had to sit quite so near each other. I kept scooting closer, but my director's chair arms were too big and I couldn't get close enough.

In the play, Man 1 through 4 are in a gym somewhere between life and death. My mother said it was a very talky play, but I liked it. She also said that no one wants to listen to four men without names debating the existence of Schrödinger's cat for an hour and a half, even if it is well written.

After Sean left, Joni immediately started talking about him, probably just so she could say his name a million times. Sean this, Sean that—Sean Sean Sean. She asked me if he had said anything about her and I said no (which was true). I told her he wanted to be in the play. I asked her if she knew that his real mom was supposed to come visit, but had to reschedule. Joni looked kind of sad and said, "Poor Sean," and wondered why he hadn't told her. I said he was probably going to but hadn't gotten around to it yet.

After the actors left, Joni and I arranged all the headshots on the kitchen table and my father walked around them slowly, thinking, I guess. We walked around slowly behind him and pointed out all the actors who were cute until my father shooed us out of the room, with "Girls, this isn't about cute, this is about character."

After we cleaned up all the water glasses and loose pages, we went to the living room and watched reruns of *Project Runway* and ate Smart Puffs. I felt sorry for this guy Malan who went home in Season 3—he said his mother thought he wouldn't amount to anything and he looked so sad and foreign. Adam kept trying to change the channel and watch *24*, but I made him stop, because Joni gets too freaked out by violent stuff.

Later, I asked my father if Sean could audition for Man 1, Man 2, Man 3, or Man 4, but he said he was looking for very specific qualities for each and he thought Sean was too young. I suggested he could be an understudy and my father said he'd take it under advisement.

I tried to do homework, but instead started writing lists:

Things Sean and I share:
Love of French
Fashion sense
We are both devout existentialists.

Things Joni and Sean share:
Rien

So, it was fate. I just wished I knew for sure how he felt about me.

I knocked on my mother's door.

"Maman, how did you know that Dad liked you?"

"Lotus, if you're having sex, make sure you use a condom in addition to birth control. But don't go on the pill—you know we have a history of blood clots in our family."

I went to Adam's room and looked at him lying there with his Game Boy.

"What do you want?" he mumbled.

"Forget it."

He looked up from the game. "What is it? Are you okay?"

I looked at Adam, and thought about asking his advice, but what did he know about love? He was only fourteen. I walked over and smoothed down his hair, which was sticking straight up.

He pushed my hand away. "Hey, don't mess with the do."

"Later, bro."

"Later, Lotus."

I went to Dad's study.

"Hey, Dad, when you and Mom first got together, how did you know you were into each other?"

He looked up from the computer. "Lotus, your mother and I, we're not getting a divorce if that's what you're asking."

In desperation, I decided to e-mail the author of *French Women Don't Get Fat* for advice. Since she was French, she probably knew all about romance.

Bonjour, Mme Guiliano!

Je suis Lotus Lowenstein and I was très impressed with your book, and I believe I have lost almost half a kilo in the two weeks I've been following the regime of French women everywhere. More important, I feel much more chic.

I have several questions I need answered tout de suite. First, can you suggest a substitute for champagne on your diet? It's très cher and I'm 15, so I'm not allowed to purchase it in this backward country. Also, what about store-bought

yogurt? Is it allowed, because, FYI, the yogurt
recipe doesn't work in this country. And most
important, could you tell me the French proce-
dure for getting a boy to embrasse you? I think
the garçon I like may be shy, but I have tried
sitting quite close to him and wearing very red
lipstick to draw attention to my mouth. So far,
rien.

Merci beaucoup.
Votre amie,
Lotus

Assignment #7
Splendid Things

*Grape-coloured material. Anything purple is splendid,
be it flowers, thread, or paper. Among purple flowers,
however, I do not like the iris despite its gorgeous colour.*
—Sei Shōnagon

The foam on cappuccino.
*When you wake up and the alarm hasn't gone off and
you have a whole hour more to sleep.*
*The feel of the grass beneath your body when you are in
the park + the warmth of someone's arm next to you as
you are looking up at the sky.*
*P.S. Ms. G, can I ask you a question? How do you
know if you are in love?*
Lotus

Vendredi, 11 Mai

So far, no answer from the *FWDGF* author.

Lotus,

I'm not sure I know how to properly answer that question. I'm afraid to admit it's been a while since I've been in love, but I certainly remember the feeling. The best answer I can give you is that you just know, in your bones, that you are in love. Regarding your assignment, I'm pleased that you chose a more positive topic and I enjoyed the poetic description, but keep an eye on the word count. Yours was a little skimpy.

How's the French club going? Any progress on the funds for Montreal?
Ms. G

five

Samedi, 12 Mai

Worked at the Wellness Center all day, read magazines and ignored Sheila, who nevertheless continued to mumble under her breath, keeping up a running commentary of everything she was doing. Like when she went to the file room, she'd mumble, "File room." When she went to the bathroom, she'd mumble, "Bathroom." I wanted to mumble, "Insane," which was where I was going.

Watched old *Gilmore Girls* reruns and studied (sort of). Also did my toenails, plucked my eyebrows, and practiced speaking French in front of the mirror. New French phrases:

Ne dis rien: Don't tell.

Ne t'inquiète pas: Don't worry.

Je meurs de faim: I'm dying of hunger.

Dimanche, 13 Mai

I met Sean to practice French conversation. Luckily, Joni was at a matinee of *American Teen* with her parents (so they could learn about what she was going through as a teen), otherwise I would have had to invite her. We went to the Chocolate Room because it's Sean's favorite place, and I had a root beer float, which was *délicieux*. Sean had an espresso and then we walked over to the Prospect Park Zoo and saw the sea lion feeding. I contemplated becoming an animal trainer instead of a journalist. There were a lot of kids, and we both agreed *jamais* on the having kids thing. Me and Sean have so much in common. We spoke in French and agreed that Joni was *très gentille* and that going to Montreal would be *vachement chouette* (very cool). I showed him my new book of French slang and we vowed to memorize it before our trip. He liked the Internet acronyms page, which has *l's tomb* (*laisser tomber*, meaning "drop it") and @+ (*à plus tard*, meaning "see you later"). Then we smoked a cigarette, passing it back and forth, and I pretended to like it, although honestly, it was pretty disgusting. I always feel so happy after seeing Sean. We are just getting closer and closer.

Lundi, 14 Mai

Ms. G,

Clarification—when you say you haven't been in love in a long time, do you mean like a couple of months long time or do you mean like years and years long time? And what was it like? And why did it end? Were you totally heartbroken? Did you contemplate suicide? Was it terribly romantic and tragic? Am I asking too many questions? It's just that I'm doing some independent research on the subject of l'amour and I believe it would be really helpful to get some data.

Also, I know my new Sei Shōnagon assignment was late, but I've been feeling very overwhelmed lately. And I've been doing a lot of thinking about raising money for Montreal, but my ideas involve activities I'm too young for, like, opening a casino or a small Campari bar. It's very limiting being almost sixteen in America.

Lotus

Dear Mme Guiliano,

Is there some very good raison you won't respond to my e-mail? I know you are très busy, but this is a critical situation. I would greatly appreciate it if you would please tell me immédiatement the secret French techniques for getting a boy to fall madly in love with you before he falls in love with your best friend. And in case you are wondering, I know he has feelings for me, because the other day, when we were doing French conversation, his arm brushed against mine and there was a total electric shock and I know he must have felt it too. Also,

he has kissed me. Oui, it's true. Okay, it was
on the cheek. We kissed goodbye on both cheeks,
to practice French greeting techniques for Montreal, but just as he was kissing me on my right
cheek, I turned my head a little so I could feel
it closer to my mouth and I know now that I am
madly in love. So, please aidez-moi.

Also, I have been following your diet religiously, and I had lost half a kilo, but now I
seem to have gained it back!!! Please advise.

Votre amie & huge fan,
Lotus

Mardi, 15 Mai

No word yet from Mme Guiliano. I read that she lived in
New York, so she should have definitely gotten my e-mail,
but maybe she was on safari and had no e-mail access. Have
to think of a way to get more money for Montreal. Even
though I've been working at the Wellness Center for what
seems like forever (actually eight weeks), I've only saved
forty-seven dollars.

Mercredi, 16 Mai

Woke up with a brilliant idea, which I mentioned at
breakfast.

"I know how I'm going to get the money for Montreal:
We're going to have a bake sale at the play."

My father looked up skeptically from his Uncle Sam
high-fiber cereal. "Lotus, I'm not sure that 'bake sale' and
'existentialism' go together."

"I'll make something relevant, Dad, a leap-of-faith brownie or something."

My mother inserted her two *centimes:* "Lotus, if you really intend to make this money, you need to come up with a more viable plan than a bake sale, and perhaps something a little less caloric."

"And don't try to borrow any money from me," said my brother, who I know for a fact has tons of money from winning all his chess matches and betting on games.

My mother frowned over her *New Yorker* and half-eaten soy yogurt. "Do you know they did a study on happiness and found that people who have too many choices are less happy? Apparently, that's why people in New York are miserable: They have too many choices of what to wear, where to go to dinner, or even what dry cleaner to use."

Dad: "So are you suggesting we move, Suki? To somewhere with limited choices?"

Mom: "I was just relaying an interesting fact."

Me: "So we'd all be happier if we lived in Stars Hollow."

Mom: "Where is Stars Hollow? Is that in California?"

Adam, mouth full of waffles: "It's a fictional town in Connecticut on that stupid TV show she watches reruns of all the time, *Gilmore Girls.*"

Me: "Eating with your mouth full is disgusting, and that show is not stupid, it's full of clever repartee. Anyway, you've watched it too, and you were, like, in love with Rory."

Mom: "Lotus, do you ever think that if you didn't watch so much TV, you'd get better grades and maybe be in better shape?"

Me: "Mom, you should talk—you watch more TV than I do. You watch *BBC World News*, Jon Stewart, *Meet the Press*, and every British mystery that's ever been recorded on public television. Anyway, I'm on a special French diet, and as a matter of fact, right now I should be eating a croissant, but we have no nutritious food here, just cardboard cereal and fake yogurt."

Mom: "It's important to stay informed of current events. And Lotus, do you know how much saturated fat is in a croissant?"

Me: "Do you know that soy isn't good for women of a certain age? I read it in *Natural Health* magazine, something about estrogen receptors."

Dad: "Please stop bickering, you're giving me a headache."

Me: "So, Dad, what do you think, *sérieusement*, about my *idée?*"

Adam, laughing like a maniac: "Lotus, that's a really half-baked idea."

Dad: "Adam, stop teasing your sister."

Mom: "Lotus, I think the bake sale is a good idea in theory, but have you considered the fact that you've never baked anything in your life—and I don't have the time to teach you?"

Me: "That's so not true. I used to have an Easy-Bake Oven and I've watched that Jacques Pépin a million times. Dad, come on, please."

Dad: "Okay, Lotus, and Suki, when was the last time you baked anything?"

Me: "I think there was a carrot cake for my birthday

party when I was seven. Although I had specifically re-quested chocolate."

Mom: "Daniel, I used to bake all the time. You just have selective amnesia."

At school, I told Joni and Sean we had to have an emer-gency French club meeting at Joni's house after school (I called in sick to the Wellness Center). I wore my new sail-boat sundress with my mother's Kork-Ease platform sandals from the seventies. I felt very South of France, although chilly. When I made my entrance, Joni and Sean were al-ready outside, by the pool, looking very chummy under one of those stripy umbrellas that I was hoping wouldn't clash with my dress. Joni was wearing stretched-out sweatpants and an old MIT T-shirt. So much for her new look.

I said *bonjour* and then kissed them both on the cheeks. Then, of course, Joni wanted to try our new French kissing thing, so she made a big deal of kissing me and then Sean on both cheeks several times. Then Joni's mother came out and sprayed us with SPF 45 sunscreen, and I told her to be *très* careful and not get it on my dress.

Sean wasn't wearing his motorcycle jacket for once—he was in a Che Guevara T-shirt with a fist on it. I know Che has something to do with Cuba and Fidel Castro and there was a movie about him, but I'm not entirely clear why peo-ple think he was so great. I told Sean it was a cool T-shirt and Joni said something about how great Che was, but I'm not sure she knew who he was either.

I shared my brilliant bake-sale idea, but neither of them seemed that excited at first. I told them about the existen-tial sayings that we could put on the cupcakes and then they started getting into the idea. We decided on "Hell Is Other People" cupcakes and "Leap of Faith" brownies, but Joni thought that "Hell Is Other People" wouldn't fit on the cupcakes. Sean suggested we do one word per cupcake like "Hell" on one, "Is" on the next, and so on.

We all agreed that that was a great idea, but I said everyone would want the Hell ones, so we decided we should make more of those. Joni thought we should make something French, but I told her that after my yogurt experience, I was pretty sure that croissants would be too hard to make and suggested French roast coffee. Then we made a budget for Montreal like Ms. G had suggested.

I wrote down three categories:

Hotel
Food
Entertainment

Joni, who has never slept anywhere except a luxury hotel, wanted to stay at a hostel, but I said wasn't it weird that the words *hostel* and *hostile* were so similar and Sean agreed it was suspicious. Joni kept insisting that it would be more authentic and I said I didn't think there was anything authentic about sleeping in a room with a bunch of German teenagers and I wanted to stay in a *charmant* inn or B&B. Joni said that I was being racist saying that the teenagers were going to be German, and I said German wasn't a race, it was a nationality. We couldn't agree, so we shelved the discussion till later.

Then Joni's mom came out and sprayed us with more

sunscreen and said she didn't want Joni to go to Canada because of dirty bombs and the border, which she says is too porous, and we had to spend twenty minutes convincing her that the border wasn't spongy and Sean said that it was Mexico you had to worry about and she seemed to listen to him.

When I got home, I did some research into hostels. They are like thirty Canadian dollars a night, while the cheapest B&B is like one hundred Canadian dollars a night, which is probably even more in American dollars, so I think we're going to end up staying at a hostel. I wonder if we'll all sleep in the same room; how weird would that be?

Lotus,

It's been a year and a half and I think I'm just now getting over it. And no, I wasn't suicidal, but I was very sad. And why did it end? Well, there's never a simple answer, but I suppose it turned out we were very different types of people and that we wanted different things. And a word of advice, Lotus—I suggest you approach your research on love cautiously, as there are a lot of dangers out in the field. On a different but no less important subject, I can give you an extension on your homework, but I expect it no later than Friday.
Ms. G

six

Jeudi, 17 Mai

Choses à faire (things to do):
Get Sean to kiss me, for real
Get Joni to fall out of love with him (and meet someone else?)
Organize trip and bake sale
Get Ms. G to go on trip with us (and get over her old boyfriend and get her a new one)

Vendredi, 18 Mai

Went to Prospect Park between school and work with Joni. We walked on the path till we got to the pond, where we sat on some benches and watched as dozens of geese floated from the center of the pond into the shallow water. Some of the geese were splashing and scratching themselves *très* vigorously.

"I never knew that geese exfoliated," I said to Joni.

"Yeah, and look at those swans," she added, pointing at a clump of swans who had just drifted over. "They look like they think they're so above it all." Joni got up and walked closer to the water. "Do you know that the correct term for a group of flying swans is a wedge of swans?"

I brushed some dirt off my shoe. "That's cool. Hey, Joni, don't get too close to that swan, I've heard they're mean."

"If my mother knew I was near any kind of bird, she would freak," said Joni, getting as close as possible to the geese without scaring them off.

I followed her cautiously. "Bird flu?"

"Yeah. The thing is, I think she's kind of getting worse. She was always really worried about terrorism and stuff, but now she barely leaves the house anymore."

"What about your dad?"

"Oh, he just works all the time. He even goes into the office on weekends, so I'm stuck with her the whole time. I've tried to get her to stop watching the news, but she's like *I need to know.*"

"I'm sorry." (I felt a little sliver of appreciation for my *maman*, who at least is not psycho.)

The swans drifted off, so we went to the Long Meadow in the middle of the park. We took out our books and lay on the grass under a tree and studied for a while, and it was kind of like old times. We talked about how fun Montreal was going to be and Joni seemed to cheer up a bit. She asked me if I thought that Sean would really audition for the understudy job on my father's play.

"Wouldn't that be cool if he became a famous actor and we all went to the Oscars and everything?"

"Yeah," I said, "that would be great." But I was really thinking that it would be great if *I* went to the Oscars with Sean, in a stunning Lacroix gown. I could see us walking down the red carpet with photographers snapping pictures and wondering who I was.

On the way home, I felt *un peu* guilty about Joni. How can I feel so close to her and yet keep such a big secret from her? Every time I hang out with her, I want to tell her about my feelings for Sean, but after what she told me about her mom today, I feel like I can't tell her, that she has enough to deal with already. As I crossed the park road, a group of bikers in black tank tops and bright yellow and red spandex shorts were gliding right toward me, fast, yelling something to one another about steroids. All of their tops had writing on them, as if they were biking billboards. They shouted and told me to get out of the way, but I just walked slower and stared at them, until they had to maneuver around me. Clumped together and chattering, they kind of reminded me of the birds at the pond. I wondered what you call a group of bikers—a barrage, maybe.

Samedi, 19 Mai

Last night there was a table read of my father's play and I got to be script coordinator. We had it in the dining room, around the big wooden table we hardly ever use. I had to clean up for an hour beforehand getting rid of knickknacks because my father wanted the room to be a blank slate. I'm taking my responsibilities very seriously and I'm even thinking I should get a T-shirt made up with my title. The actors all just said their lines and didn't act much. On breaks, they smoked cigarettes and acted bored. It was very exciting. My job was to make sure that everyone had water and didn't miss any of their lines, although they were reading from the script, so they really didn't have any excuse to drop lines. During the actual performance, I am going to be the prompter, so I will get to stand in the wings and help them out when they forget their lines. I can't wait. During the reading, I had time to examine the cast in more detail.

Man 1: middle-aged with glasses, but nice, shook my hand. My father said he was the everyman type. I think he might be good for Ms. G. I have to find out what he does for a living.

Man 2: very cute in a rumpled actor way. My father called him the male ingénue. I think he looks like Johnny Depp.

Man 3: pretentious, with a fake British accent. Wore a billowy white poet shirt. Sort of attractive in that older guy (40s) kind of way. Called me Lo (FYI, this has never been my nickname). Then annoyed me further by calling me *Lo darling,* as in, *Lo darling, could you get me some iced tea with lemon.* My father said he has lots of experience. I'll bet.

Man 4: really old (50s? 60s? 70s?) philosopher type, also with glasses. (I consider him a possible suitor for my *grand-mère.*) He was very polite, although he went to the bathroom three times and I began to wonder if he had a prostate problem. I sort of drifted off during the monologues, but I'm sure the play is brilliant because my dad wrote it.

After the reading, the actors scattered and my father seemed really happy and nervous. He was talking really fast like he had drunk too much coffee or something. "Do you realize, Lotus, that there's only six weeks till the production? It's unbelievable. I can't believe it's really happening. How are we going to get everything done? Oh, by the way, your friend Sean called me; he wants to be the understudy."

"You're kidding. So, Dad, are you going to let him?"

My father paced back and forth, muttering something I couldn't hear. "Lotus, it's a lot of memorization. Do you think he's up to it?"

"Oh yes, totally. He's really smart: He takes AP English."

"Okay, Lotus, since he's your friend . . . but I'm counting on you to make sure he memorizes every line."

"Thanks, Daddy. You're *très* super." I went to bed imagining Sean and me hanging out in the theater together, studying his lines late into the night, and his speech at the Oscars thanking me. I thought about the swans and the bikers and decided a group of actors could be an accolade of actors.

Later, Sean called to tell me he got the understudy job, which I already knew, but I pretended it was the first time I had heard it and acted really excited, which I am. It's a hard job being an understudy. He basically has to memorize the entire play so that if one of the Mans gets sick, he can take over.

I went to Sean's house to give him the script. He lives in a duplex apartment with his father and stepmom, not a brownstone like me and Joni, and it's all very *Architectural Digest* with giant modern paintings with slashes of paint and those Mexican rugs whose patterns can give you a headache. I was thirsty, so he made some lemonade with real lemons and snips of mint. I told him that it was delicious and just like a French citron pressé, not that I've ever had one.

We sat on opposite ends of the long white couch and I studied my French slang and Sean studied his lines for a while (*Ce mec me branche* means "I like that guy" and *J'ai fait la traverse du désert* means "I haven't had sex in a long time"—how true, like, my entire life). After a while, we got really sleepy, so he asked if I wanted to lie down on the bed and rest. My heart was beating really fast, but I was like, sure, as if I lie in bed with boys I'm in love with all the time.

He lay on his back on the bed and put his hands over his head and immediately fell asleep. I lay on my side, wide awake, facing him, and closed my eyes, but then I opened them a little so I could watch him from under my lashes. He has the most beautiful arms (golden with tiny golden hairs) and I scooted a little closer to him, and in his sleep, he scooted a little closer to me, until the entire length of our bodies was touching, which felt amazing.

I think I must have drifted off to sleep for a moment because when I opened my eyes he had gotten out of bed and was on his computer and I was sprawled across the entire bed. I hoped I hadn't been drooling or making weird noises while I was sleeping. My skirt had totally ridden up, so I pushed it down and jumped up off of the bed and said I had to get going. Sean said, "So soon? I kind of like having you here, sleeping."

"How long was I asleep for?" I asked casually, trying to smooth my hair back into place.

"I don't know, twenty minutes?"

I felt *très* awkward as if I had taken off all my clothes (in French slang, you say *mis à poil*—literally translated as "I'm only wearing my body hair," gross), but I hadn't—they were on me, just all wrinkled. We *bised* (kissed) goodbye and I left quickly so I could go outside and stand there for a bit and savor the experience of having slept with Sean, sort of.

Dimanche, 20 Mai

I called Joni and she couldn't talk because Sean was over there studying his lines. She sounded so thrilled to be helping him. I told her I was the official script coordinator and that I should be there, but she said she knew I had to work and everything, that was why they hadn't called me. Right. Then she whispered that she thought Sean liked her, although nothing had happened, it was just a feeling she had. When she said this, I felt like someone had punched me in the chest. Could Sean really like Joni? Had I been imagining all the feelings between us?

Met Sean and Joni at the Chocolate Room after I got off work. Joni was all *Remember when we were here last time* to Sean, but he just acted normal and said that the chocolate cake was amazing. I was in the mood for chocolate fondue, though, so we decided to get that. Then I thought about Sean and me lying in bed together and I started to feel warm and I glanced over at him to see if he was remembering it too and he winked at me when Joni wasn't looking.

The fondue came with marshmallows and fruit and slices of pound cake, which we dipped into the bubbling chocolate with our wooden sticks. As we were all leaning over the fondue pot and laughing about the pieces that fell in, I thought about how Jean-Paul Sartre and Simone de Beauvoir both shared a romantic relationship with the Russian girl Olga, but I wasn't sure I was sophisticated enough to share, and after reading about it, I'm not sure Simone was that happy about it either. They seemed to only be able to love each other through these other people, which was messed up.

Assignment #8
Things That Arouse a Fond Memory of the Past

It is a rainy day and one is feeling bored. To pass the time, one starts looking through some old papers. And then one comes across the letters of a man one used to love.
—Sei Shōnagon

The taste of a pain au chocolat, or someone telling you that they like having you around, giving you a warm feeling that you carry around inside you for days.
—Lotus Lowenstein

Lundi, 21 Mai

VERY NICE, LOTUS! I LIKE THE MOOD YOU CREATED.
Ms. G

seven

Mardi, 22 Mai

Ms. G,

Glad you liked the assignment. I've been giving your situation a lot of thought and I've decided that you really need to get back on the cheval, so to speak, and start dating as soon as possible before you get out of practice. And whatever you do, don't get a cat—it sends the wrong signal to guys.

FYI, we are moving along really fast on the Montreal planning and I will be sending you the budget shortly. We are having a bit of a debate about whether to stay in a bed-and-breakfast or a hostel, but since we don't have much money, I think we're going to end up at a hostel, and hopefully it won't be full of annoying tourists or serial killers like they always are in the movies. I wouldn't blame you if you wanted to stay in a charming B&B and just come visit us.

BTW, I'm really counting on you coming with us. As you mentioned, if we want to get any school funds, we have to have a chaperone. Also, if there's any hope of Joni's mom letting her go, we need to have an adult with us, to protect us from roving terrorists and hurricanes. I don't think my parents are worried, and Sean said his parents don't care what he does as long as he gets good grades. Also, I've heard the garçons in Montreal are très cute (hint hint).

À bientôt,

Lotus

Bonjour, Mlle Lowenstein,

I was very happy to receive your letter and know that you are enjoying French Women Don't Get Fat, which is a huge success on both sides of the Atlantic. While I can't answer each letter personally, I would like you to know that your thoughts are very important to us and have been forwarded to the appropriate department for review.

If you would like more individual attention and support, I suggest you sign up for the monthly membership on the FWDGF Web site.

Bonne chance et bon appétit!

Mireille Guiliano
French Women Don't Get Fat

Chère Mireille,

I hope you don't mind if I call you Mireille, but I feel so close to you, I took the liberty. Thank you for your lovely form letter. I understand that you are très occupée and don't have le temps to answer each letter personally, but I feel my situation deserves your special attention. First the bad news: I have gained 1.5 pounds. Perhaps it's Evian weight. I wanted to sign up for your online program, to get the extra support, as you suggested, but I don't have a credit card (ma mère est très stricte) and also can't afford the $19.95/month fee. Do you offer a student discount?

On the amour front, things are progressing rapidly, and I feel that my relationship is about to get plus physical, but I'm feeling a little guilty about my best friend, who is in love with him too and knows nothing about our assignations. Any pensées?

Also, I'm a huge fan of Veuve Clicquot champagne, so if you have any samples, please send tout de suite.

À bientôt,
Lotus

Samedi, 26 Mai

My *grand-mère* and I went to MoMA (that's the Museum of Modern Art). It's weird how the only people you see when you go to museums are tourists. They are easy to spot by the digital cameras they insist on using at every opportunity. They must be given cameras in the airport and forced to document every second of their trip for immigration purposes. My *grand-mère* said she didn't think you were allowed to use cameras in museums, but I read a sign that said still photography was okay. *Moi*, I think cameras are for making art, not taking pictures of art.

Our first stop was the café. This is the first thing we always do in a museum: Go to the café and rate the food and ambience. My *grand-mère* says this is the true mark of a museum—that and, of course, the bathroom. The Brooklyn Museum, for example, really needs help with the café—it's in the basement and the food is cafeteria style (*Mais non!*).

I had trouble deciding between the *assiette de fromage*, which comes on a large wooden board, and the arugula salad (healthy). I ended up getting a portabella and fontina panini (delicious), after asking one of the cute guys who works there what was good. He told my *grand-mère* to watch out for me and I said my *grand-mère* is the wild one and everyone went *ha-ha*. My *grand-mère* had an apple brioche and coffee. Two little girls behind me were calling the artisanal flatbread matzo and I turned around to correct them although they didn't really seem to appreciate my wisdom. I asked my *grand-mère* how the red hat ladies are going. She told me that she likes hanging out with them, but that she wishes she had a man to spend time with.

"Just to have dinner with, Lotus, no moving in. I'm done with picking up after some man."

She told me she was thinking of trying speed dating—

apparently they have one for the over-sixty-fives, but instead of three minutes a person, they get five.

Art advice from Lotus Lowenstein:

Walk quickly through the museum and let the art rush over you. Never get the audio thing, and don't spend too much time reading the descriptions.

Step in front of people taking pictures—they need to realize they are in the way.

Museum wardrobe advice: dress comfortably yet fashionably— you are not trekking through the Himalayas. Leave the Birkenstocks and backpacks at home.

When I got home, I wrote a letter to the museum.

Dear MoMA,

I just wanted to let you know that the use of cameras in the museum significantly detracted from my experience of your museum, which I enjoyed overall. I especially enjoyed the Rothkos, the Cornell boxes (you should get more), and the whimsical Duchamps in the Dada area (très existential). However, I don't want to pay $20 (actually, my grand-mère paid) for Japanese tourists to shove cameras in my face. FYI, my grand-mère is partial to the Edward Hoppers, so keep those. Other suggestions: more shade on the terrace, and please put in seats at the espresso bar on the second floor. People are walking all over a museum, they're tired, they don't want to stand. On a more positive note, we thought Café 2 was delicious. We're not fans so much of the communal *tables, but we went early, so it was fine. I look forward to your response on the camera issue.*

An art lover,
Lotus Lowenstein

Dimanche, 27 Mai

Breakfast. My father was making blueberry pancakes. *Quelle surprise.* I think the last time we had blueberry pancakes was when my *grand-père* died.

"So, who died?" I asked.

"Lotus, don't be maudlin. No one died, I just thought it would be nice." My father flipped a pancake.

"*Quelle* relief. Hey, Dad, I have another moneymaking idea for the trip. A raffle. We can do it at the play."

Mom said, "Lotus, your father's play isn't all about ways to make money for your trip. It's about the play."

Dad said, "The-thing-in-itself. Do you know that's a philosophical term, Lotus, *the-thing-in-itself*. From Kant. Originally, it comes from the Greek *Nooúmenon*."

"Hmmm. That's really interesting, Dad, but do you have anything you could raffle? An acting lesson or a directing lesson or a playwriting lesson or a philosophy lesson or something?"

He slid some delicious-looking blueberry pancakes, dripping with butter and syrup, onto my plate. "There you go."

"Wow, those look great, *merci!*"

"Well, how about a playwriting tutorial, Lotus? Just be sure to limit the time. Let's say, two hours."

"Great, thanks. And how about you, genius boy?" I reached over and tickled my brother. He smelled like potato chips and laundry detergent and I almost had the impulse to give him a hug.

"Cease and desist. Well, I suppose I could give a few chess tips."

"Thank you, thank you, thank you." I tried to hug Adam, but he told me to get off before he called Child Services.

"Hey, Mom, do you have anything I can raffle? Joni's mom is donating an emergency disaster kit with a crank radio that you can charge your cell phone with when all the power goes off."

"Lotus, that woman needs help."

"The raffle, Mom?"

"Give me a moment to think about it, Lotus. And do you really need that many pancakes?"

My brother stuck his plate in my face and I slid a small pancake from mine to his.

"Lotus, give some more to your brother. Okay, I have a thought. Why don't you ask at the Wellness Center if they would donate some services? It would be good publicity and could bring in some money for you. Talk to Barbara."

"I guess I could. . . ."

"Okay, now that you've gotten all these donations, Lotus, why don't you donate some of your time and clean up the kitchen?"

"What about Adam?"

"He's got chess this afternoon."

Everyone fled the kitchen, leaving me with a ginormous

pile of dishes to wash, like I was a waif in *Les Misérables*. I was okay with it, though, because it gave me time to think about my relationship with Sean. There were *problèmes*, of course, like the fact that Joni likes Sean, the fact that I still haven't told her about my feelings for him, the fact that I haven't heard from him in days, but as I knew from literature, all great loves have obstacles.

Lundi, 28 Mai

Yesterday afternoon Sean called and asked me to come over after work and help him with his lines. They've been rehearsing at the Unitarian center where my parents are members. Unitarianism is like a religion for people who don't believe in religion but they still want to get together and do group things.

The wait for work to be over was endless. Sheila was making disgusting hacking/sniffling noises due to sinus problems (*dégueulasse*). Even with headphones, I couldn't drown her out. Then, a woman with the most annoying child I've ever seen expected me to watch it while she had a Reiki session for her irritable colon. The kid kept lying on the floor and screaming until I finally gave him a *Vogue* to tear out pages from, which seemed to keep him quiet. When the mother finally came back, she said she didn't want him exposed to that sexist trash. *Incroyable!* How could any mother not think *Vogue* is educational?

Finally, I was released from prison and went to Sean's. We rehearsed in his living room, which has huge open windows and very clean, slightly uncomfortable square furniture that looks like it came out of a fancy catalog. Sean played Man 1 and I played Man 2 and then we switched so he could learn both parts.

Man 1 (*walking on a treadmill*): *I am looking out at scenes of the Pacific Ocean on my individualized state-of-the-art computer screen. I am perfectly content, this is exactly where I want to be at this moment. It's very Zen.*

Man 2: *Do you have any idea what time the gym closes?*

Man 1: *Closes? What do you mean? It's open twenty-four hours. It never closes.*

Man 2: *How long have you been here?*

Man 1: *Quite a while—more than a while. Maybe two whiles. I'm not sure; I've never actually thought about it. But check out these machines. They tell you everything: how many calories you've burned, your GPS coordinates, the precise location of the twelfth moon.*

Man 2: *There are twelve now?*

Man 1: *Just turn to CNN—you'll learn all about it. It's fascinating.*

Man 2: *But what about the pool? It's never open.*

Man 1: Oh, it'll be opening soon. A continuous wave pool. Very elegant, very technical. Everyone's talking about it.

After we went through like ten more pages, I got bored. "We should take a break and celebrate."

"What?"

"You getting the understudy part."

"And us going to Montreal," said Sean, putting down his pages.

"And being friends."

"Cool."

We started searching for something festive to drink. His house was so entirely different than mine. Everything was in its place, not scattered around, no mandalas or pictures of the early Beatles staring at you all the time. Instead, there were framed photographs of giant waves and underwater flowers, like it was the lobby of a fancy hotel or something. The house even had a smell that reminded me of a hotel, a faint hint of flowers or some special room spray.

"Do you even have parents?" I asked him. "Or were you raised by cleaning bots?"

Sean laughed. "Definitely bots."

"Oh yeah? So where are they, these bots?"

"Being serviced."

I searched through the glass liquor cabinet and picked up a bottle of some strange yellow liquid that looked like a potion. Sean yelled from the kitchen that he had found a bottle of champagne.

"*J'adore* champagne," I yelled back.

"*Moi aussi.*"

"Won't they kill you, *tes parents?*"

"No, they'll never notice—I'll put another one in the fridge, *plus tard.*"

Sean popped the cork. It flew across the room in a small explosion and golden champagne bubbled out. He grabbed some skinny glasses and we clinked them together.

"To Sean, the famous actor."

"To Lotus, who is adorable."

Then we lay on one of the perfect couches in the living room and pretended we were the queen and king of some small French-speaking island. Sean was the king and I was his queen.

"Darling, can I pour you more champagne?" he murmured.

"*Oui, mon chéri.*"

"I wish J.P. were alive so we could invite him over," said Sean, making a toast.

"Do you know that he and Simone de Beauvoir always called each other by the formal *vous*, not *tu?*" I added.

"That's so weird. I would always call you *tu*."

"Me *too*. Get it?"

We drank more champagne and got sillier and sillier. It reminded me of the time my parents had a Day of the Dead party and I drank all the leftover margaritas out of their glasses as I was cleaning up, until they found me and threatened to send me away to Unitarian camp. I put my legs across Sean's on the couch and he started playing with my feet. He said they were cute. (Thank God I gave myself a home pedicure recently.)

"Hey, stop, that tickles."

Then Sean started tickling me for real (I'm very ticklish). Soon, we were laughing and punching each other with pillows and messing up the perfect couch and throwing all the giant pillows on the floor.

Sean kept tickling me and tickling me until I couldn't breathe and finally I rolled on top of him like I used to do with my brother, trying to pin down his arms so he couldn't get to me. But instead of stopping, he pulled me down and kissed me. A real kiss, not just a peck or a *bise*, a real fullfledged, French-movie-star kiss. When we rolled apart, I felt kind of stunned. We drank more champagne and we didn't kiss again, although I wanted to. We didn't talk about it, just went back to rehearsing the play, but I know that things will never be the same.

Mardi, 29 Mai

Afterward, *après la* kiss, everything looked the same, but was different. There was BSKM (Before Sean Kissed Me) and ASKM (After Sean Kissed Me). Everything in the world is brighter now, more colorful, the edges of things are sharper.

Went to school. And work. And home. I ate dinner (veggie burgers and chocolate pudding), but all I could think about was Sean Sean Sean. Why didn't he call? I kept going over to the phone and picking up the receiver to make sure it was working and then feeling like an idiot. At one point, Adam was on the phone to one of his nerdy friends talking about video games, and he wouldn't get off. Sean probably tried to call at that exact moment, but because *mes parents* don't believe in cell phones or call waiting, I'll never know. I've tried to explain to them how they're ruining my life, but they don't get it.

Mercredi, 30 Mai

It was a beautiful afternoon in the neighborhood and I was not going to think about why Sean hadn't called me. Anyway, we are so close that we are in touch in a way that transcends phone lines. The sun was shining and I was making *French Women Don't Get Fat* vegetable soup and I felt thinner already. Adam came into the kitchen while I was chopping exotic French vegetables like turnips and parsnips.

"Lotus, what the hell is that smell?"

"*Mon* handsome *frère, ça va?*"

"Studied Spanish, remember?" He picked up a turnip and took a bite.

"I was just saying, 'Hello, how are you, my handsome brother?' Those are raw, by the way."

"Oops." He spit the turnip into a napkin. "What are you making anyway?"

"Vegetable *soupe de Maman.* It will be *très délicieuse.*"

"Why are you in such a good mood?"

"That's for me to know and you to find out. And what about you—where are you going all dressed up? Are you actually wearing a tie?"

"Regional chess championship." He yanked his tie off center.

"Are you going to win?"

Adam shrugged. "I'm hoping to come in third."

"Still, the parents must be thrilled." I stirred my soup vigorously.

He leaned against the wall. "I guess, I don't know, I'm kind of tired of all this chess stuff."

"I know—you need to be free and unfettered."

"You said it," Adam muttered. "See you later."

After many hours and much food processing and much spillage (luckily *Pierre le chien* seemed to like the soup), my mother wandered into the kitchen.

"Lotus, you're going to clean all this up when you're done, aren't you?"

"*Oui*, Maman. Hey, Maman, who was the first boy you kissed?"

"Joel Rothstein." She leaned over the blue Le Creuset pot of soup with a dreamy look in her eyes. "We were in shul together. He had the most amazing lips." She picked up a spoon and tasted the soup. "Not bad, Lotus, not bad at all." She threw in a little sea salt without asking my permission. "Maybe we'll have some for dinner later when your dad and Adam get back."

Dear Mireille,

I just made your vegetable soupe de Maman. You may not realize this, but most American households do not own a food mill. In fact, most Americans (including moi) have no idea what a food mill is. I was forced to use a food processor to make the soup and judging by the mess, it was not the ideal implement for the job.

I also have to let you know that, sadly, most Americans do not eat turnips. In fact, I had never seen them before. Nevertheless, after many hours of chopping (we don't have servants, either), I finished your soup and I have to confess it was superior to every other soup I have had and I felt amazingly full after just two bowls. I used sour cream instead of crème fraîche—I think you should suggest that in your next book. Otherwise, I am still in love, and Sean and I have even kissed, and it was very romantique and we will probably be living together in Paris very soon.

Your amie américaine,

Lotus

After I wrote to Mireille, I studied essential French slang.

Où se trouve la cabine d'essayage? Where's the fitting room?

J'ai flirté avec lui: I made out with him. (I studied this one a lot.)

Quoi de neuf? (in e-mail: KOI29): What's new?

Later, when Adam and Dad came home (Adam placed third as he predicted, although I was kind of surprised he hadn't come in first), everyone ate my soup and admired his trophy. Then Adam and my mother disappeared upstairs and my father and I had some coffee ice cream in the kitchen.

"Hey, Dad, *quoi de neuf?* How's the play going? Do you need me to do any more script-prompting stuff at rehearsal—whip them into shape?"

My father patted me on the head absentmindedly.

"No, Lotus, it's fine. They need to be off-book in a week or so anyway, so I don't want to give them a crutch."

"How's Sean doing?"

"Good, he's been coming to all the rehearsals. He's a very nice young man. Very reliable. Everyone likes him."

"I know." (I felt proud, as if I had invented him.)

When I went up to my room later, my mother had left me a bunch of condoms and an ancient copy of *Our Bodies, Ourselves*. Some of the drawings were quite disturbing and hairy. After a restless night of sleep, I realized the reason that French women don't get fat is that they have to get up five times during the night to go to the bathroom.

Jeudi, 31 Mai

Still haven't heard from Sean since the kiss. I'm trying to feel secure in our love, but it would be a little easier if he would call me. I just have to believe in him, and remember our kiss, and not let doubts overtake me. Joni and I have been hanging out a lot. She's totally taken over all the Montreal planning and has an Excel budget file on her computer. Yesterday, we went to the DSW at the Atlantic Terminal Mall. I tried on some Prada shoes that were divine but cost $259. *Je ne crois pas*. I ended up getting some silvery flats for $19.99 and Joni got a pair of espadrilles.

"Those are cute," I told her.

She pointed her foot out in front of her. "I think Sean will like them."

"Definitely. Who wouldn't? They are chic—you could wear them in Montreal."

Over peanut butter fudge ice cream at Cold Stone Creamery, I tried to prepare Joni for finding out about me and Sean by telling her about how Simone de Beauvoir refused to let jealousy change her relationship with Sartre. "And I think Jennifer Aniston should have just accepted that Angelina Jolie was better for Brad and moved on a little more quickly. If she had, I think all of her relationships since would have worked out better. I mean, after all this time, she's still not happy."

"Well, maybe she thought he was her soul mate."

"Maybe, but you can't own people."

"I guess not."

"I feel sorry for her."

"Jennifer, yeah, me too."

I hope Joni doesn't think of Sean as her soul mate, because they really don't have much in common.

After ice cream, Joni and I came up with the idea to henna our hair. Henna is this ancient magical powder that Cleopatra used to color her hair. The good news is that I think mine came out pretty nice, a kind of European darkish red, but the bad news is that I don't think Joni is ever going to talk to me again.

Everything was going fine at first. Joni's parents were at an autism benefit, so we went over to her house and watched *America's Next Top Model* and pigged out on potato chips full of trans fats and Kraft onion dip and then I told Joni about my idea for writing a book called *Everything I've*

Learned in Life I've Learned From America's Next Top Model. My first chapter would be "The Girl Who Complains About the Other Girls Always Goes Home," because there is always one girl who is really mean, but instead of that girl going home, the girl who complains about her is voted off. Joni said we should also have a chapter called "The Girl Who Gets Her Hair Cut Short Always Goes Home." This is the girl who every season goes mental after they chop off all her hair and even though she usually looks much better, the girl never believes it and then she loses all her self-esteem and whines nonstop and the judges vote her off. We practiced our runway walks up and down the hallway and made fun of Tyra Banks and the bizarre robotic way she describes the prizes. We were having fun, like when we were little and would have sleepovers and make our Barbies do fashion shows and stripteases. Then we got out the henna powder we bought at Back to the Land, the natural-foods store, which my father calls "Back to the ATM" because everything in it is so expensive. Joni's mother says that hair dye causes breast cancer, so we bought the expensive organic henna powder. I let Joni mix it up because she's a science genius. While Joni mixed the powder with warmed lemon juice, I put on one of her mother's old Fleetwood Mac records and we danced around to "Go Your Own Way."

"Hey, what does pancake batter look like?" Joni asked. "That's what it says in the directions, that it has to have the consistency of pancake batter."

"I can't believe you've never made pancakes."

"Have you?"

"No, but I know what it should look like: thick but not too thick."

We put the batter on each other's hair, really carefully, because her mom's bathroom has all these pink marble tiles and we didn't want to stain anything or have henna necks. We both wore gigantic yellow rubber gloves that cracked us up. Then we sat in the bathroom, Joni on the corner of the bathtub, me on the teak towel bench, as we waited a million years for the henna to penetrate our hair shafts.

"We're going to look so great for our trip, aren't we?" I said. "All those Montreal *mecs* will go wild."

"What's a *mec*?" asked Joni, scratching under her turban.

"That's slang for a guy."

"Oh. You know, Lotus, we're really going to have to figure out the money. When Ms. G comes to the next club meeting she's supposed to let us know how much money we can get from the school and then I can add it up on my Excel spreadsheet, and then we'll really know if we can go."

"We can't *not* go! I need to be surrounded by people who don't speak English who will understand me."

Joni was studying the lanky model on the henna package. "Hey, do you think Sean will like my hair?"

"Sure."

Sitting there with Joni, I suddenly felt horrible, like I was split in half. Half of me was her friend, and the other half was in love with Sean. Both parts of me couldn't listen to her talk about him anymore and not say anything.

"Listen, Joni, there's something I have to tell you. About Sean. Before you get too—"

"Wait, wait, wait—I need to go first." Joni came and sat next to me on the little bench.

"Okay." I couldn't sit still, so I got up and paced back and forth in front of the sink.

"We kissed." Joni paused dramatically and adjusted her turban.

I stopped moving and looked at her. "We who?"

"Me and Sean, of course."

Of course. *Bien sûr.* Sean kissed Joni. Sean, who kissed me, had kissed Joni. That was why he didn't call. He liked Joni. He didn't like me. I peeled off my yellow rubber gloves and pulled at the sticky yellow fingers.

"Lotus, are you okay? You look weird. Do you think you're allergic to henna?"

I felt sick, like the time I got food poisoning in Rhode Island after eating some bad clam chowder. "I'm fine. Do you know, in French the word for kiss is the same word as the slang for having sex? *Baiser.* Weird, huh?"

"Yeah, I guess. So what do you think about me and Sean? Are you surprised? And what did you want to tell me about him anyway?"

Joni looked so happy that in my mind I was yelling, *Don't tell her, don't tell her, don't ruin everything,* but the words just started coming out of my mouth. It was like in those movies where someone is possessed by an alien.

"He kissed me, too."

Joni stared at me from under her white turban like she

had never seen me before. It was then that I realized I shouldn't have said anything, but I couldn't take it back. And yet at the same time, I felt a weird relief that I wasn't keeping this giant secret anymore.

"Look, Joni, I wasn't going to tell you, but I think I should be honest, and you should know what he—"

"It's not possible."

"Joni, it just happened."

She glared at me. "That's so lame. A *tsunami* just happens. A kiss doesn't just happen."

"Okay, okay, I guess I wanted it to happen. But I didn't plan it. And you kissed him too, so I thought you'd understand."

Joni laughed, but in a harsh *it's not funny* kind of way. "But you knew how I felt about him. I can't believe that you listened to me all those times I told you all my personal feelings! What were you doing, just pretending to care and then going after him behind my back? Some best friend. You couldn't stand that he liked me better because it's always all about you. I can't believe you, Lotus!"

I didn't know what to say. I felt like sinking down, past the pink bathroom tiles, into the middle of the earth. The truth was that I hadn't even thought about Joni when I was kissing Sean. I had only thought about Sean.

"It's not like that, Joni. And it doesn't have to be the end of everything. Simone de Beauvoir and Sartre both had relationships with the same women and they stayed close until the end."

"Don't start telling me about Simone de Beauvoir and

Jean-Paul Sartre and their stupid open relationship, because I really don't care at the moment."

"Joni, I'm sorry."

I tried to touch her arm, but she was maniacally cleaning up the bathroom, spilling henna paste everywhere. She looked kind of insane, with the giant towel still wrapped around her head, and the bathroom smelled horrible, like a chemistry lab. Joni kept trying to scrub the henna off the tiles, but it wasn't coming off.

I put my hand out and touched her on the arm. "What do you want me to do?"

She shoved my hand away. "You've done enough already."

"Joni . . . ," I pleaded.

"Lotus, I can't even look at you anymore. You should just leave."

So I left. I walked home without even taking off the big white towel that was on my head. I was crying for a while before I even realized it. Joni and I had had fights before, but nothing like this. The way she looked at me, like she hated me, was awful. I thought about the first time she came over to my house and yelled at my brother for teasing me, and how later we made a secret pact to always be friends. And how we had planned to go on double dates with our boyfriends (when we finally got them). And later, when Joni was a famous scientist and I was a top journalist with a chic white trench coat, move to New York and share a fabulous apartment. And then I thought about Sean, Sean kissing Joni. I kept seeing it in my head, his beautiful face leaning in to hers. Why did he kiss her anyway? Did he kiss every girl he came in contact with, or was he just being nice? Or did he really like Joni better than me? Should I just give him up and let Joni have him? Or was it too late anyway? All these questions were swirling around in my head like I was on a game show and I started running just to get away from my thoughts.

When I got home, I ran to the bathroom and rinsed out the henna and put Joni's mom's towel in the sink. As I rinsed it out, it looked like blood was running down the drain.

Vendredi, 1 Juin

I got up with a feeling of dread. I wore all black. I left a note on Joni's locker saying I was very sorry and I hoped she could forgive me. During the day, I saw her once, outside her advanced bio class, but she just looked past me like I didn't exist. The day sucked. I didn't bring in my homework for English and Ms. G asked me if I was okay and I almost burst into tears. As I was leaving class, she told me she was looking forward to coming to our Montreal planning meeting next week.

After school, I didn't know what to do with myself. I was almost happy when it was time to go to work. At the Wellness Center, Sheila was in a weirdly good mood. She had met some guy on the Internet and they were sending each other jokes and YouTube videos of cats doing kooky things and she was going to meet him for a first date. She commented on my hair, but didn't say she liked it, just, "Oh, your hair is different." I said, "Thanks a lot," as if she had told me she liked it. Why do people do that? If you don't like it, just don't say anything. I told Sheila that she should make sure this guy was who he said he was because there are a lot of weirdos on the Internet, but she didn't seem concerned, probably because a weirdo was exactly what she was looking for. She then proceeded to tell me about the disgusting meal she had planned for her dream date, which involved beans and tempeh and a Crock-Pot.

At dinner, my mother and father didn't notice my hair, which was a *très* noticeable shade of red, nor my mood, which was quite dark. The only thing they noticed was that I wasn't eating my food. I poked at the poached wild salmon my mother had made and tried to eat it, but the black skin and the filmy white coating underneath were making me feel sick.

"Lotus, don't pick at your food," said my mother.

"Mom, I thought you'd be overjoyed that I'm only picking at my food, since you're always saying I eat too much."

"Your mother worked hard on this meal, Lotus," lectured my dad, "and the least you can do is try to enjoy it."

My mother made flirty eyes at my father over their slimy pink slabs of salmon.

"At least eat some salad, Lotus," said my father.

"You know I hate beets."

"Lotus, I thought you had outgrown these childish food issues."

"Well, I haven't."

My mother turned to my dad. "Remember when we were

at that little restaurant in Nantucket and I couldn't bear the thought of oysters?"

"I know, and then you loved them."

They laughed and then my mother leaned over and kissed my father. My life was over for all intents and purposes, and my parents were practically having sex at the dinner table.

I interrupted them. "Hey, did anyone call me?"

My dad squeezed lemon on his salmon. "No, sweetie, I don't think so."

No, of course no one called. Did I think that Joni would actually still want to be friends after what I did? That she would call me? Ever? Or that Sean would call? I'm sure Joni has forgiven Sean. Right now they're probably kissing and talking about what a bad friend I am. My life is over. *Fini.* After dinner, my mother brought out a chocolate cake. I think it was the first time in my life that the thought of having dessert made me want to throw up.

"What are we celebrating?" I asked.

"Your father got a grant. For his play. I knew you would, honey." My mother made googly eyes at my father.

I raised my eyebrows at my mother, who had never believed in my father's play at all, but she ignored me. Of course, now that he had gotten the grant, she was being nice to him. "That's great, Dad. Way to go."

"It's a small grant, but it will pay for the sets and maybe there will be something left over for publicity."

"Hey, Dad, can I come to rehearsal tomorrow?"

"Lotus, honey, you know I'd love for you to be there, but

we're into the heart of the rehearsals and I need to create a culture of safety for the actors. So I've decided to close the rehearsals to outsiders."

"Okay, okay, whatever."

I went to my room and played Edith Piaf's "Non, Je Ne Regrette Rien" and considered whether I regretted kissing Sean. I thought about it for a few minutes, but the answer was no. I regretted Joni hating me, but I couldn't regret Sean, and especially not the kiss. It was the single best moment of my life. I picked up the phone a dozen times to call him and then finally dialed. His cell phone went straight to voice mail, so I decided to call his house. A woman answered, his stepmother, I guess, or the housekeeper. The other times I had called I had only gotten the answering machine, so I guess this was progress.

"Is Sean there?" I asked, trying to sound casual.

"Is this Portia?"

"No, it's Lotus."

The woman sounded a little embarrassed. "Oh, sorry, no, Sean is out."

"Could you tell him I called?"

"Of course I will. Lotus, right?" Now she sounded like she felt sorry for me.

"Yes, Lotus. L-O-T-U-S, like the flower."

Who the hell was Portia? When I got off the phone, my first impulse was to call Joni and talk to her about this new girl in the picture, but then I remembered she never wanted to hear from me again. Maybe Portia's just some girl from Sean's other school, a friend or something. Maybe it's nothing. Or maybe he really likes her. I don't know what to think, and even worse, I have no one to talk to about it. Joni was the one I always told things to, and it really hurts not to be able to anymore.

Dimanche, 3 Juin

Woke up feeling happy and then remembered how messed up my life has become. I'm all alone: no best friend, no boyfriend, no one to confide in. Everything is *merde*.

Then I thought, *What would Mireille from* French Women Don't Get Fat *do? What would Sei Shōnagon do? What would Simone de Beauvoir do? They certainly wouldn't lie around feeling sorry for themselves.*

I got up and carefully picked an outfit for a day alone without any friends or boyfriends or life to speak of. I put on a bright red T-shirt dress I had gotten at the Gap, tied a blue scarf around my neck, and slipped on my retro espadrilles with the ribbons that tie around the ankles.

I decided to go to the library. In the back of my mind, I was thinking I might run into Joni and try to get her to forgive me. I wandered around the library, looking at the books other people had reserved, which were all on a big shelf, organized by the name of the person who had asked for them. Amy Sohn, the girl who used to have a column about sex in the *New York Press*, had requested two Montessori books (how dull and family-oriented), and Paul Auster (a scary-looking writer my father likes) had requested a book called *The Brief and Frightening Reign of Phil*, which sounded sort of interesting. I switched their reserved books around, but even that didn't cheer me up.

After the library, I went to the park. Everyone there was part of a couple or a family, or else a crazed exerciser. I was the only one in heels. I felt Mireille would have been proud of me. I took some photos of leaves and imagined having a big photography exhibit at the Brooklyn Museum. Joni and Sean would come. By then, they would be married and living in Park Slope with twins, and I would look fabulous and be living in Paris. They would be tired and covered in baby goop, and Joni would wish she had stayed friends with me and Sean would wish he had answered my phone calls.

When I got to the pond with the swans, I threw them some baguette crumbs I had in my pocket until a woman started yelling at me that I wasn't supposed to feed them because it disrupted their natural cycle and they would die in the winter after losing the ability to hunt for their own food. I ignored her, but she had ruined the moment, so I turned around and went back home.

I never realized the day had so many hours in it. I had gone to the park and the Botanic Garden (where dozens of Asian couples were getting their wedding pictures taken), and it wasn't even noon yet. The day seemed endless. One bridegroom had purple spiky hair and looked like he had come straight out of an anime cartoon. On the way home, a cute guy came up to me and tapped me on the shoulder. I turned toward him and smiled. He was pointing at my shoes and I wondered if he was going to compliment them.

"Your shoe is untied," he said in an accusatory way.

I stopped smiling and glared at him. "Thanks, but you know what? I was kind of enjoying them being untied."

The guy looked away, like I was insane. It's so annoying the way people are always telling me to tie my shoes, or zip up my pocketbook, or smile. *Mon Dieu*, it's like living in a police state. When I got home, I was so exhausted I had to lie down on my bed and eat some Camembert until I revived.

"Hey, Lotus." My eyes were closed, but I still recognized the annoying tones of my brother.

"Didn't you ever hear of knocking, Adam?"

"Some guy is on the phone for you. Should I tell him you're in a coma?"

I jumped up. "No, no, I'll get it. *Merci, merci, merci!*"

It was Sean, *Dieu merci*, and we talked, and his voice sounded so relaxed and normal that I know everything is going to work out. He still likes me. He said we needed to talk, In Person. I was thrilled. When I hung up the phone, I ate a madeleine and tried to figure out what Sean wanted to TALK about. The Kiss? Joni? Us? *L'amour*? While I was falling asleep, I imagined us kissing again and then how we'd run away to some exotic island where no one could find us.

Lundi, 4 Juin

When I got to the Chocolate Room, I stopped and looked at Sean through the window. I felt like I was in a play, meeting someone I hadn't seen in years. He was studying the tiny brown menu as if it had been written by J.P. himself. I hurried inside to his table and he got up and we kissed on both cheeks. The café smelled delicious, like hot chocolate and coffee and fudge all mixed together.

I ordered hot chocolate with extra whipped cream and Sean got an espresso and we ordered a piece of chocolate cake to split.

We talked about nothing for a little while. I told him that in French e-mail, MDR is the same thing as LOL, except it means to die laughing, *mort de rire*, instead of laughing out loud. We talked about the boredom that is school, and how thrilled we were going to be to get out soon.

"When I called you the other day, your mother thought I was some girl named Portia," I said to him, *très* casual, when our cake came.

"That was my stepmother, not my mother."

"Sorry. But who is Portia?"

"Oh yeah, Portia. She's a good friend of mine, from my old school. We still get together sometimes. She's really smart. I think you'd really like her."

"I'm sure I'd like all your girlfriends," I said, smiling warmly, although I felt cold inside.

"She's not my girlfriend." He said this so seriously, it made it sound like she *was* his girlfriend.

"Okay, okay, whatever. This cake is really good, isn't it?"

"Yeah, it's great, but look, Lotus, the thing is, I really don't have time to be in a serious relationship with anyone. I've got school and the play and your father's been giving me all these philosophy books to read. I'm reading a book now called *Irrational Man*, by William Barrett." He pulled a small green volume out of his back pocket. "It's amazing. You've got to read it, Lotus."

"Oh, definitely." For a moment, I wanted to take the

book and throw it at him, but then I decided that jealousy was not an emotion I wanted to indulge in. Portia was just a friend and I had nothing to worry about. Anyway, he was with me now, not Portia.

We sat there for a moment sipping our drinks and then Sean looked at me like he was seeing me for the first time. "Hey, I like your Eiffel Tower earrings." He leaned over and touched one, making it swing back and forth.

"Thanks." My ear felt all warm on the spot where his finger had been.

"Can I ask your advice, Lotus?"

"Of course, *bien sûr*."

He leaned in again and I felt kind of weak. Is that what *l'amour* is, some kind of flu that overtakes you until you're too weak to resist? It seemed like a long moment before he said anything, and I held my breath.

"It's . . . it's just that I don't know what to do about Joni. You know, we fooled around a little, but she's not, she's not cool about it like you. I think she thinks we're, like, together or something. She keeps calling me."

The words *cool about it like you* floated around my brain in a good way and a bad way.

He thinks I'm cool about it, but he's also talking about Joni, and comparing what we did to what they did. What did that mean? And then I thought, *Poor Joni*. She would be so upset if she could hear him.

"Well, you know, she hasn't had much experience with boys."

"Yeah, but . . ."

I don't know why I felt angry on Joni's behalf, but I did. "She really likes you, Sean, and she probably thought you liked her too."

"Hey, I do like her—she's really sweet. But Lotus, you know that I'm trying to live a life of complete freedom, like J.P."

I couldn't disagree with that. "Of course you are. So am I."

"Do you know what he said about love—that it's either sadism or masochism?" Sean looked at me like that explained everything.

"Well, I guess, but—"

"Let me read you something from *Irrational Man*. He's talking about Sartre's philosophy here: 'The lover wishes to possess the beloved, but the freedom of the beloved (which is his or her human essence) cannot be possessed; hence the lover tends to reduce the beloved to an object for the sake of possessing it. . . .' Isn't that great?"

While he was reading, I was looking at his hair and the way it fell in his face and I kept wanting to touch it. "Yeah, that's amazing."

"You and I, we're the same kind of people, Lotus, but Joni's more sensitive. I'd really appreciate it if you could say something to her . . . like about how she needs to back off a little."

"I don't know—that would be kind of weird, because of what happened . . . with us."

"Yeah, I suppose." Sean shrugged, as if that weren't a valid reason.

"And we're kind of having a thing right now, me and Joni, a disagreement."

Sean looked down at his phone, which was vibrating in a nasal way. "She's already called me three times today."

"You should call her back. Hey, if you want to go over to her house now, that would be okay with me. I've got some stuff to do, anyway."

"See, that's what I mean about you—you understand about personal freedom."

We sat there for a while and I asked him questions about *Irrational Man* and told myself that this was exactly the kind of life I was looking for: deep intellectual conversation with someone who is free. I pushed all thoughts of Joni and Portia out of my mind with each small bite of cake.

When Sean left, he kissed me on the mouth, leaving me weak and totally confused.

I went home and asked my father if we had any absinthe, but he just laughed and patted my arm. I lay on my bed and tried to *comprends* what Sean had said to me, about how cool I was with us fooling around. Does that mean if I am cool about it, we'll do it again? *Am* I cool about it? Or do I want to possess him and take away his essence? I wonder if he went over to Joni's after he left me. She definitely wants to possess his essence. And I can't blame her. If I had to choose, I'd rather he was with Joni than Portia. What kind of a name is Portia, anyway? I know it's from some book we did in school, but I can't remember which one. *Mon Dieu*, it's difficult to be an existentialist in love.

Hours went by in contemplation of my problems and the meaning of life (actually twenty minutes), and then my mother came in and sat down on my bed. For once, I was happy to see her and I decided to ask her advice since she's always bragging about how many boyfriends she had before she met my father. But before I could say anything, she picked up one of my fringy throw pillows and hugged it, saying, "Lotus, I want you to be extra nice to your brother right now, since he's going through a difficult time."

"What do you mean?"

She started punching the pillow I had paid good money for at Anthropologie. I grabbed it back from her before it was destroyed.

"Whoa, Mom, relax. Breathe. What's the *problème?*"

"Where have you been, Lotus? Mars? Adam lost his chess match yesterday. I'm sure I told you. The Super Regionals. The big one. He didn't just come in second or third, which would be acceptable. He was decimated. Never even made it to the finals. Can you imagine how he must be feeling?"

"Yes, I can. And no, no one told me." I felt strange about Adam, both worried about him and relieved that, for once, I wasn't the screwup.

"So I just want you to be extra nice and supportive."

"I'm always nice to him."

"Don't give me a hard time, Lotus. And maybe you should get up and take a walk before dinner. It would do you good. You can't just lie in here like an invalid for your whole life."

After she left, I decided to lie down on my bed like an invalid for my entire life. *Pierre le chien* came to lie down with me and I tried to ask his advice, but he just fell asleep. Why do I always have to worry about everyone else's *problèmes?* When are they going to start worrying about mine?

At dinner, we had all my brother's favorite foods—fried chicken, mashed potatoes and gravy—ordered from some new Southern restaurant. We even had lemonade for an authentic touch, although my parents were drinking it with a shot of bourbon for additional authenticity. My mother had an article from the paper in front of her and was arguing loudly with my father about something to do with Iraq, even though he was nodding and seemed to be agreeing with her.

I looked at the pool of gravy on my mashed potatoes and tried to scrape it off. Everyone knows I hate gravy. "This food is so American, it's going to ruin my diet," I complained.

My mother looked up. "Lotus, remember our conversation."

I looked over at my brother, who did not seem decimated. On the contrary, he was tearing a piece of fried chicken apart with great enthusiasm.

I said, "Hey, Adam, sorry about your match."

"No worries, mate. I've got it all sorted. I think I'm going to join a band."

"Let me guess, a British-inspired band."

"Yeah, the London Eye. It's named after this awesome ride they have over there."

"I know. That's a good name."

My parents stopped talking about Iraq and, in unison, turned to my brother.

My father: "Adam, what are you talking about? It's just one match. You can't quit."

My mother, sputtering through her mashed potatoes: "Do you know how much money we've spent on chess, how many matches I've gone to, and now you want to start a band? Are you kidding me?"

My brother, chomping on a wing: "Look, guys, I'm fourteen now. I need to do something real, not this geeky chess stuff. Dad, I thought you'd understand. You're an artist."

I couldn't believe that Adam had the guts to stand up to them! I wanted to cheer him on.

"Yeah, Dad, you should understand how he feels," I added, "being an artist and all."

My father glared at me. "Be quiet, Lotus." He turned his disappointed face to my brother. "Adam, I didn't think you were a quitter."

My mother softened a bit. "Adam, do you want to see someone to talk about this?"

"It's not drugs, is it, son?" asked my father, wearing his concerned face.

Adam stood up. "No, Mom, I don't want to see someone, and no, Dad, I'm not a drug addict. I just need some space." With that, he grabbed his half-chewed wing and a biscuit and left.

What is it with men and space? Then my parents turned on me, like a pack of wolves. "Lotus, that was really not helpful," said my mother.

My father said, "Lotus, do you realize what an important moment this is in Adam's life?"

"What, what did I do? It wasn't *moi* who quit chess. And what about the fact that Adam seems perfectly fine?"

"You encouraged him. A band, for God's sake. Anyone can start a band, but Adam has a real talent—he could have had a chess scholarship, he could have been a champion."

"Dad, what about freedom? Isn't that what you're teaching Sean about, freedom of choice and all that philosophy stuff?"

My father coughed. "I just don't want Adam to regret this later."

I wanted to bolt too, but I forced myself to keep sitting at the table and continue scraping my mashed potatoes until they were totally free and clear of gravy. Then I ate the skin off my chicken breast. My parents sipped their drinks and looked heartbroken, like someone had died. To break the tension, I tried to change the subject.

"Dad, do you think that love is really either sadism or masochism?"

"Lotus, this isn't the time. Your mother and I need to strategize."

I left the table. No one seemed to care. I glanced in at my brother to see if he was okay, but he had his Bose headphones on and was tapping out a rhythm on his desk with some pencils. I imagined my brother as a rock star and me as a rock journalist with one of those laminated backstage passes around my neck, meeting all kinds of rock stars and famous people, and looking cool in my knee-high shiny black boots.

I lay in bed and tried to ignore my parents arguing with Adam. When they were gone, I went back to the kitchen and made magic leek broth from the detox section of *French Women Don't Get Fat*. I drank two cups of magic leek broth. Then I did some homework, in between going to the bathroom 5,000 times from the magic leek broth.

Things J'adore
Lying in bed doing nothing for the rest of my life.
Hot chocolate with extra whipped cream.
Cheese.
Sean.
Days when it is warm enough to wear a T-shirt, but not hot enough to sweat.

Things Je Suis Upset About
My best friend never speaking to me again.
J.P. Sartre, for making the person you're close to think it's okay to be with a bunch of girls at once.
My father, for giving that person books to read about Sartre.
Portia (even though I don't know her).

Cher Mireille,
    Being French, I think you are the seule personne who can help me. My friend Sean, the boy I told you about, is trying to be like J.P. Sartre and be with a bunch of girls, not at the same time, but still. I'm all for freedom and existentialism, but I can't help feeling not so bien about it, and my friend Joni is totalement in love with him. She is already traumatisée after finding out that he kissed me, but if she found out about Portia, who

is this girl from Sean's past who may or may not be his old girlfriend, I think it would be beyond tragique. Plus, I'm worried that I'm a masochist. Plus, we're all going to Montreal together soon and we are still not speaking! With all of the stress, I've gained 1.5 kilos. Don't worry, I am continuing to drink magic leek broth to detox.

Hope you're not offended by my criticism of J.P. Sartre, but how did Simone de Beauvoir put up with him anyway? And what should I do?

Votre amie,

Lotus

eight

Mardi, 5 Juin

French club meeting. We met at school in the library. Ms. G was all excited and told us that she had found us money in a school slush fund that would cover our train tickets and hostel stay—all we'd need to get was money for our food and incidentals. She asked how much money we'd raised and Joni said that was my department, and I said I was working on the Wellness Center to donate some services we could raffle.

"What about the idea of a bake sale at your father's

play?" asked Ms. G. "I thought that was a better idea. Are you still doing that?"

I looked at Joni, but she looked away.

"Definitely. We're working on it."

I tried to seem excited about the trip, but it was hard to imagine spending three days with Joni who was so obviously not talking to me. She could barely look at me, and whenever I said something, she stared in the opposite direction. Ms. G gave us permission slips to get signed by our parents. She asked Joni to make the train and hostel reservations and Sean and I were supposed to come up with cultural activities.

"And you're studying your French, right?" We all nodded.

I told Ms. G about my slang dictionary and I taught her how to say "I need an eyebrow wax," which she needed to know because she has these very bushy eyebrows and waxing would open up her whole face. Ms. G just laughed and said that we could only hit the salon after we'd had several educational experiences. Sean asked if we were going to hear some jazz and Joni looked at him adoringly.

As we left the meeting, I said to Joni, "We're going to have to figure out what we're doing for the bake sale. Are we still making the existential cupcakes?"

Joni looked right through me. "I don't care. Just e-mail me what you want me to do." Then she grabbed Sean's arm and they walked away.

Mercredi, 6 Juin

It was only two weeks until the end of school and I was in *l'enfer*, which is the French word for hell. I was in love, had four finals, two papers, and no Joni. My father's hair had gotten all wild and he kept pacing back and forth muttering about how the play was going to be a failure, how they were never going to be ready, how no one would understand what he was getting at, how American theater was in the toilet. He was also keeping Sean away from me with endless rehearsals. Both the parentals were still mad at Adam. Like a good cop–bad cop team, they took turns pleading with him not to throw his life away and scolding him. Other times, they ignored him, as if they were in one of those religious sects that shun people. By default, I had become the favorite and they were actually asking my opinion about things, like what we should have for dinner. I made a delicious *Gratin à la Normande* the other night that even my mother loved after I told her it was made with low-fat cheese and soy bacon, which were total lies. (It was made with pancetta, heavy cream, and an entire Pont l'Évêque, which I had to go to three different cheese stores to find.) Adam had been banned from dinner so he could think about his life, so we had plenty of leftovers. As an international journalist, I think it's important to have a repertoire of simple dishes that you can whip up behind enemy lines.

After dinner, I went to Adam's room to see how he was doing. He was eating potato chips, wearing a Dead Kennedys T-shirt, and practicing something called paradoodles with his drumsticks on a small rubber pad since he doesn't have actual drums. "I'm going to be the next Ginger Baker," he told me.

"Who's he?"

"Are you kidding? He was one of the greatest drummers ever: Cream, Blind Faith. Do you know that he used to insist that his drums be nailed to the floor when he played?"

I picked up a chess piece that was lying on the floor and put it back on his desk. "No, I didn't. Hey, what's this one, the crook?"

"No, the rook."

"I knew that, I was just testing you."

"You think I'm doing the right thing, Lotus, don't you?" he asked me, putting down the drumsticks for a second.

"Well, of course you shouldn't get trapped in some bourgeois lifestyle if you're an artist," I said. "Besides, some of those chess kids were pretty dorky."

"Here, listen to this." He made some loud, annoying noises with his drumsticks.

"Great paranoodles!" I told him, wanting to be encouraging, despite the fact that he seemed to have no musical talent whatsoever. "I'd love to hear more, but I've got tons of studying to do."

Jeudi, 7 Juin

I truly believe that my coworker Sheila could have a successful career as a hypnotist, because sometimes when she's standing in front of me and talking, I start to fall into a trance. I made the mistake of mentioning that I had made

Gratin à la Normande from *French Women Don't Get Fat* and she began describing one of her own culinary masterpieces, tempeh pot roast. She is one of those people you tell something to, and they immediately start telling you something boring that they've done that you didn't ask about. I have never eaten either tempeh or pot roast and I want to keep it that way. I told Sheila that I only believed in eating fresh food from the market and that I had read an article in *Natural Health* that said that fermented foods led to yeast problems.

Samedi, 9 Juin

Ms. G and I went to Sephora yesterday after school. It wasn't a plan, I just ran into her in DSW, where she was trying on some really ugly sensible shoes, which I made her put back on the shelf. She didn't want to go with me to Sephora, but I told her that it would be educational and that I needed to talk to her about my paper. It was like a whole new world to her. She may know a lot about Jane Austen and Proust and symbolism, but she doesn't know anything about bronzer, eyeliner, and lip gloss. At first, she acted all anti-makeup, as if wearing foundation were like doing crack cocaine. I had to reason with her.

"Haven't you heard of global warming? Don't you know it's essential to have a layer of something between you and the sun? Look, this one even has sunscreen."

We walked around the entire store because I know how important it is to get just the right makeup person to help you. "We need someone who really knows cosmetics," I whispered to Ms. G, "not some fake-tan, shimmer-stick addict who wears Jessica Simpson perfume." I pointed at a victim of *Us Weekly*. Finally, I saw a tall blond transvestite wearing heels and bright red lipstick. I whispered to Ms. G, "That's the one."

Ms. G frowned. "Lotus, isn't she a he?"

"Uh-huh, she's perfect. Don't worry, I know what I'm doing. She looks good, right? Like a glamorous woman. You'd never know that she was a he except for the hands and the Adam's apple. That's what we're looking for—real skill."

I gave Bianca, our beauty consultant, specific instructions for making up Ms. G. "I want super sophisticated, but not over the top. In fact, I want her to be wearing so much makeup she looks like she's wearing no makeup at all."

"Yes, yes, yes, I totally see what you're going for," said Bianca, staring down at Ms. G. "I love a blank slate."

"If I'm going to be looking like I'm wearing no makeup, then why bother?" asked Ms. G.

Bianca and I shook our heads at her naïveté.

"You'll see," I said.

Bianca was great. She was young and glamorous, with a totally retro look. She told me she liked my personal style (I was wearing my stripy espadrilles, navy sailor pants with all the buttons, and a red halter top). She let us try on a zillion different brands: Stila, Chanel, Fresh, Benefit, and Bare Escentuals. Bianca and I decided that Ms. G was a Laura

Mercier type of person because she liked all the neutral color palettes. After twenty minutes of our pleading with her, she agreed to let Bianca put her in the makeup chair and apply foundation, blush, eye shadow, and some lip gloss. But she held firm on no lipstick or mascara.

"I'm just not that type," she told me, as I tried on some individual false eyelashes with glue from Bianca's makeup kit.

"Okay, no lipstick, but give her a lot of gloss, Bianca."

When Bianca was finished, she twirled Ms. G around on the makeup chair and showed us what she looked like in the large lighted mirror.

"She looks like a movie star," I said to Bianca.

"Girl, with the right haircut, she could be Julie Christie. Not that you know who that is."

"From *Shampoo* and *Don't Look Now?*" I asked nonchalantly.

"Definitely *Shampoo*. How do you know about those old movies? I thought I was the only one who watched them."

"My family has movie night every Friday. We went through a whole seventies period."

Ms. G kept looking at herself in the mirror and touching her face. "I just don't know if it's me."

Bianca gave us our basket of products, pointed us to the cash register, and hugged us goodbye. She told us she did a cabaret show on Tuesday nights at Don't Tell Mama and we promised we'd go see her. I knew that Don't Tell Mama was a club because I'd been there once with my dad and his gay friend Damien to see a Judy Garland impersonator. The show took place in a small, dark room with uncomfortable chairs, and, as soon as we sat down, a chunky waitress with very short hair demanded to know what drinks we were going to get, because there was a two-drink minimum. I ordered two cranberry juice and sparkling waters with lime, which the waitress said was the AA special.

For a moment, I contemplated Bianca becoming my new best friend and giving me significant discounts on makeup, but then decided she was great but no Joni. As we wandered through the perfume section on our way to check out, Ms. G seemed to read my mind. "Lotus, is something going on between you and Joni? You two didn't appear very close at our last meeting."

I snorted. "You can say that *encore*. I guess we've grown apart." I sprayed myself with a fragrance called Dirt, which smelled exactly like dirt, but in a good way, like going to a farm or something.

"May I ask what happened?"

"It's *compliqué*," I said, not wanting to tell Ms. G about Sean and the kissing and everything. "So how about you, Ms. G, any luck on the dating front?"

"I'm still not sure I'm ready, Lotus."

"Oh, you're ready."

When we got to the cash register, Ms. G was shocked that her purchases added up to $186.

"You can't put a price on beauty," I told her. I got the saleslady to give us free perfume samples, which makes everything in life a little easier. After we left the store, we were exhausted and had to get coffee at Starbucks. I got a double mocha with whipped cream; Ms. G just ordered a tall decaf. The guy behind the counter asked Ms. G if she would like a sample of their cinnamon latte muffin. When we sat down, I said, "Did you see the way that guy looked at you? He was so into you. I bet it's your makeover."

Ms. G whispered, "Lotus, you're imagining things. He was just doing his job."

"He didn't ask *me* if I wanted a muffin sample, so I had to take my own," I said, eating my three tiny samples.

Ms. G sipped her decaf. "I hope you and Joni will be getting along on the trip. I wouldn't want you to miss out on anything because you're fighting."

"Don't worry, we'll be fine. Hey, can I ask you a question?"

"Of course, Lotus, you can ask me anything."

"How important do you think monogamy is in a relationship?"

Ms. G looked a little shocked.

"It's not like I'm sleeping around or anything, it's just . . ."

"No, you're right, Lotus, it's a valid question. To me, it's essential, but I can't speak for anyone else." She paused. "To be quite frank, I believe that infidelity is a very destructive force in a relationship. That was what happened in my last relationship."

"Oh, wow, I'm sorry, Ms. G. Here, have some more muffin."

"No, it's okay." Ms. G played with her wooden stirrer, breaking it in half. "It's not even the infidelity itself—it's how foolish you feel having trusted the other person."

Dimanche, 10 Juin

Yesterday, I took the subway up to Central Park to meet my *grand-mère* for Walk for the Cure. I was wearing my comfiest wedge sandals, a pink Puma T-shirt for breast cancer awareness, a white tennis skort, and a red headband for the red hat society. There were all these people on the subway reading religious texts. I read *Vogue*, which is spiritual in its own way.

When I got to Central Park, I couldn't believe how many people were there. Hundreds of runners were milling around, stretching their legs in their tiny shorts and showing one another their hideous outfits. I waited on the L–R line to get the ugly number that I was supposed to safety-pin on my chest. I wrapped it around my wrist instead.

I finally saw my *grand-mère* and her ladies, who could be identified at a distance by their red sea of hats. My *grand-mère* gave me a big hug and introduced me to all the ladies, whose names I immediately forgot. Everyone gathered around me like I was a minor celebrity. They immediately started bugging out about my outfit.

"Lotus, don't you want to change into sneakers?"

"What, she's not wearing sneakers?"

"You're wearing *those* for the race? Oy!"

"You can't walk in that outfit, young lady."

"Where's your red hat?"

I tried to calm them down. "Okay, one at a time, please. I didn't wear sneakers because A, sneakers wouldn't match my outfit, and B, I don't own any. And I'm wearing a red headband. Any other questions?"

They told my *grand-mère* I was delightful and had such

an adorable figure. I wanted to tape their comments and play them back to my mother. After some waiting around and some power stretching, the race began. We walked for what seemed like an eternity. Soon, I had finished my entire bottle of water, a power gel, and a Luna bar.

"*Grand-mère*, how many miles has it been? I feel like I'm being tortured."

Everyone laughed like I had made a great joke. "It's only been a quarter of a mile, Lotus."

I couldn't believe it. I felt like I had been trudging in the Sahara for miles and miles.

"I'm never going to make it. How do you *do* it?"

"Lotus, you know that I walk two miles at seven every morning from Bloomingdale's to Gramercy Park. You should try it."

"I'd rather not."

"You know Simone de Beauvoir used to go on long walks, tramping through the woods for hours," said my *grand-mère*.

Another woman piped up. "That's true, Lotus. Our book club just discussed that new biography about her and Sartre called *Tête-à-Tête*. We had French cocktails and Sylvia made a baked Brie."

"But what about those contingent relationships?" asked a short, plump lady wearing a red baseball cap, a glittery pink sweat suit, and pink sneakers.

"Contingent relationships? What do you mean?" asked a skinny lady in a white tracksuit.

"That's the fooling around," said Pink Sneaker Lady, adjusting her bra strap.

Soon they were all talking at once:

"And did you see what he looked like?" said a lady with unnaturally bright red hair.

"Small and ugly," said another one, giggling.

"Like my Morrie," said White Tracksuit Lady, putting her hand over her heart.

"That poor Simone de Beauvoir," chimed in a lady with a frilly red headband, pumping her arms while she walked.

"Yeah, he was a dog," said Pink Sneakers.

"And he didn't even like sex," said the redhead, sniffing loudly.

"It's always the woman who gets the short end of the stick," said White Tracksuit, who was trying to walk and take her pulse at the same time.

"That free love is for the birds," said Pink Sneakers.

"But they made a choice to share everything," I said, panting, trying to catch up. "To be free!"

"That's true," said my *grand-mère*, taking my side. "And would she have written all those wonderful books without Sartre?"

"Maybe she would have written even more brilliant books if she had a husband who appreciated her," said Pink Sneakers, passing us on the left. We were approaching a hill and I think I had already developed blisters on every one of my toes. I tried to slow down, but the ladies just yelled at me to keep up.

My *grand-mère* said, "Well, Lotus, I'm sure your young man, if you have one, is nothing like that ugly little Jean-Paul Sartre. He was brilliant, but the thing is, it's important to separate the idea from the man. You don't sleep with an idea, you sleep with a man. An idea doesn't buy you flowers or take care of you when you're sick. Your husband does." Her voice sounded funny.

"Are you thinking about *Grand-père?*" I asked her.

"Every day, Lotus, every day."

Lundi, 11 Juin

Last night, Sean and I took a walk. He kissed me three times: once at the corner of First Street and Seventh Avenue, once outside the G & Y deli (the one we call the GAY deli) after he came back from getting cigarettes, and once as we sat on the same side of the table at the Joyce Bakeshop, eating cheese straws. I was kind of worried that Joni might be around and see us, but Sean told me not to worry about her. When I went to pay for the cheese straws, the girl behind the counter said, "You should let him pay for that," but I said I didn't believe in that kind of old-fashioned, sexist stuff. Then I asked her how much it would cost to get custom cupcakes. She said it would cost $3.50 a cupcake, so unless we charged $4.50 for each existential cupcake, we would make nothing. I asked Sean if he wanted to help me practice making cupcakes but he said he had rehearsal.

He paused. "I thought Joni was going to help you."

"Yeah, I'm going to call her. I just haven't gotten around to it." I did want to call Joni. Every day, I thought about calling Joni. I just didn't know what to say.

"By the way, I wanted to thank you for talking to her. It really helped."

I didn't know what he was talking about. I hadn't talked to Joni, and why would she say I had? But I was curious, so I decided to play along.

"No problem. What did she say I said to her?" I couldn't wait to hear this.

"Nothing specific, but I know you must've said something, because she's so much more relaxed now."

"Great." I said, trying not to sound sarcastic.

Under the table, Sean pressed his knee into mine. "I really wish I could stay, but I've got to go back to rehearsal. Your father's freaking out about the blocking."

"Yeah, he's been going mental at home, too."

"Hey, you know my father and stepmonster are going away for a couple of days this week, so maybe you could come over."

"Yes, that would be *incroyable*." I couldn't believe it. I was finally going to be alone with Sean and I could find out how he really felt about me. I wanted to believe in free love, but what I really wanted was for Sean to tell me he only wanted me, not Joni, not Portia, not anyone else.

Mardi, 12 Juin

There's only one week left of school. I've gotten through half of my finals and written one-third of my paper on the diary form, titled "Diaries, Real or Embellished?" I'm using excerpts from various diaries like Anne Frank's, Bridget Jones's, mine, and, of course, Sei Shōnagon's. I think

Ms. G will love it, and not just because I helped her with the makeover. I wonder if she'll notice if I triple-space it?

Reading Anne Frank's diary was too upsetting and all the crying was ruining my makeup, so I had to stop writing my paper and take a brief cupcake break. She was so brave. Here's what Anne F. said about writing: "When I write, I can shake off all my cares." That's so true. I think we have a lot in common. Reading about Anne F., I suddenly felt angry with Joni for being so petty about everything, when we could all be killed tomorrow. I took a bite of my cupcake and wondered if Anne Frank ever had a cupcake and then started crying again.

```
to: joni222@yahoo.com
from: lotusfille@hotmail.com
```

Joni, I know you're not speaking to me, but we really have to deal with the cupcake issue. Unless you've decided not to go on the trip to Montreal, which I could totally understand as it might be très awkward if we are still not speaking to each other.

Back to the cupcakes: I've been to Joyce Bakeshop and Two Little Red Hens and that other new bakery on Seventh Avenue, but all their cupcakes are way too expensive ($2.50 to $3.50), so if we sold them for $2, as planned, we would lose money on every single cupcake. I assume you still don't want to get together and bake them, even though that would make the most money and I'm becoming an excellent chef. Do you have any other pensées? And BTW, have you ever read Anne Frank's diary? It's very moving. Life is so short, n'est-ce pas?

No response.

I have to admit, I was kind of surprised that she didn't write back. I kept checking my e-mail, but there were only jokes from my grandmother and my French-word-a-day e-mails (I learned that the word for "toad" in French is *crapaud*, which sounds entirely disgusting). Since I didn't hear from Joni, I attempted to bake cupcakes on my own.

Here's what I learned. Apparently, measuring is really important. And if you don't have an ingredient, let's say baking soda, you can't really substitute another ingredient, like flour, for it, or else the cupcake will taste really weird and even *Pierre le chien* won't eat it. Make sure you grease the pan or buy those little paper cupcake holders so your cupcakes won't stick to the pan. Otherwise, even after soaking, your pans will still take like an hour to clean.

Since my time is very valuable and could be much better spent doing things other than slaving away in a kitchen, I decided I would have to outsource the cupcakes.

```
to: joni222@yahoo.com
from: lotusfille@hotmail.com
```

Okay, fine, don't help. Whatever. I've spent hours doing research and finally found a bakery that will do the cupcakes for $1 each, including decoration, if I order 100. The bakery is called Mrs. Maxwell's and it's in some scary part of East New York, Brooklyn. They were really nice, though. Their motto is "It's not a real party if you don't have a Mrs. Maxwell's cake." So, I've calculated that if we sell the cupcakes for $2.50, we'll make $1.50 each. I'm also thinking we could put a jar out for donations for our trip so that diabetics and people on a diet who

can't eat cupcakes could still contribute. It
could say something like "Help Send Culturally
Starved Brooklyn Teenagers to Montreal for Educational Trip." We also have to pay Mrs.
Maxwell's $10 for delivery, because my father
says it's too dangerous to go there, not that
you'd care if I get killed by urban violence. How
many do you think we should get? I'm thinking
1,000, because everyone will eat at least 3.

Still no response. I'm getting kind of tired of this. I
mean, okay, I kissed Sean, but it's not like I'm a Nazi war
criminal or made Joni die in an attic.

```
to: joni222@yahoo.com
from: lotusfille@hotmail.com
```

I talked to my dad and he said the theater holds
100 people, so I think we should get 100 cupcakes. If there are leftovers, we can just sell
them the next night. What do you think? I have
to make a decision here and I could use your
input if you're not too busy. Also, how many
chocolate ones do you think I should get, as opposed to vanilla, and how many vanilla ones with
chocolate icing as opposed to chocolate with
vanilla icing? These are important decisions
and I could use some help!!

Still no response.

```
to: joni222@yahoo.com
from: lotusfille@hotmail.com
```

Okay, fine, be that way. I'm ordering 100 mixed
cupcakes, but I still need $110 on delivery. Any
thoughts on where we can get the money? Hint,
hint. Also, I need to know if you're coming to
the play so I can reserve a ticket for you. If
I don't hear from you today, I will assume you're
not coming.

Mercredi, 13 Juin

This morning, I found an envelope under the door with a check for one hundred ten dollars. No note, so I guess we're still not talking, but there is communication, of a sort, which I think is a positive sign.

Jeudi, 14 Juin

Sean invited me to come over after school to help him with his lines. It started off so *romantique*. When I got to his house, he took my hand and walked me upstairs to his bedroom without saying a *mot*. It was wonderful, and I felt very French. It was mostly kissing and kissing and kissing and a little rolling around on the bed. While he was lying on top of me and kissing my neck, it felt so *fantastique* for a moment, but then I started to get a cramp in my left foot. Then we heard some noise, which was his parents returning early from their trip. At this rate, I will probably remain a *vierge* for my entire life like Joan of Arc. I rushed to the bathroom to brush my hair and try to look normal. His parents were very slow bringing their stuff into the apartment, so we had time to run downstairs and pretend we had just been sitting on the couch, studying. Later, I realized I had left one of my Eiffel Tower earrings somewhere in his bedroom.

His stepmother is *so* not how I pictured her. I was expecting someone fit, because of all the Bikram yoga she does. She is *très* thin, but she looks more like one of those ballet ladies, you know, the ones who wear their hair in a bun and turn their feet out like ducks. Sean's father is tall and serious and barely spoke to me, just disappeared to make a call. I asked his stepmom if they were going to the play and she acted like she had never heard of it, so I told them it was going to be quite the event and that it was a philosophical thriller, like *Waiting for Godot* meets *Silence of the Lambs,* plus there would be cupcakes. She looked at me as if I were insane, and said something about checking their schedule.

"My father got a grant for this play. It takes place in a gym in a very nonlinear way."

His stepmother pointed her foot and stared down at it. "Well, we'll try to go, but this month is tricky."

Sean walked me to the door, but he seemed kind of annoyed.

"I can't believe you told her."

"Told her what?"

"About the play. I wasn't going to tell them," he whispered.

"Why?"

"I just don't like them to know what I'm doing."

"I'm sorry, I didn't know." I felt like an idiot for telling his stepmom about the play, but at the same time, why *wouldn't* he tell his parents? It's a totally amazing play and they're lucky to have the opportunity to see it.

We couldn't kiss goodbye because his stepmother was there, so I just left.

Jeudi soir

On the very important night of the dress rehearsal, I wore a black sweater and a black skirt. I also carried a very efficient clipboard with the script on it so I could prompt the actors with their lines. There were a bunch of people I hadn't seen before, including a masculine girl named Lorrie who was the stage manager/lighting person and a very thin and elegant costume/makeup guy named Luke. They were both chain-smoking cigarettes and badgering my father.

"There's not enough time for the costume changes," Luke complained. "It's a disaster."

"And those pathetic exercise props are not going to make it," growled Lorrie.

My father moaned, "Just make it work, guys. If you need anything, triage with Lotus." He pointed at me. Immediately, Lorrie and Luke gave me a bunch of annoying errands to do, like going to the hardware store and the sewing store to buy tons of Velcro, pins, and lightbulbs.

When I got back, I bumped into Sean, literally, and he said he needed to talk to me, as I was picking up all the packages that I had dropped. He stooped down to help me and we bumped heads again, this time gently. He led me to a nook outside the dressing room. I was sure that he wanted to talk about us, but instead he whispered, "Your dad's having a meltdown in the dressing room. We've got to do something."

"Okay." Didn't he even remember our recent romantic moment? Am I that forgettable?

We went in. My father was sitting with his head in his

hands, moaning. I pressed acupressure points on my father's wrists to try to calm him down and Sean gave him half an Ativan that he had taken from his stepmom's medicine cabinet.

"What's this?" asked my father, staring down at the pill like he had never seen one before.

"Just something to help you relax, Mr. Lowenstein. Very low dose. My stepmom takes them when she flies."

"I am relaxed," said my father as he swallowed the pill. "I'm just having a little trouble reconciling myself to the fact that tonight is going to be the beginning and the end of my theater career."

Man 1 came into the room and started coughing.

"Are you even going to be able to speak tomorrow?" demanded my father. "You sound like death."

"Of course I'll be able to speak. I'll be perfectly fine," croaked Man 1, before dissolving into another coughing fit.

"Hey, Camille, don't ruin your costume," said Luke to Man 1. "If you're going to be sick or cough up anything, take it off, okay?"

"Who is Camille?" I asked, confused. "His name is Frank."

"Camille from the Dumas novel," said my father. "Very apropos—she died of tuberculosis in a garret."

"Look, I know Man 1 backward and forward," said Sean eagerly, "so if he's sick—"

"Just stab me in the back, why don't you, Eve Harrington?" said Man 1, exiting dramatically with one last hacking cough. Sean followed him to study his gestures.

"I get it, Eve Harrington from *All About Eve,* the one who tries to sleep with Bette Davis's boyfriend and steals her part. Okay, Dad, this is my best Margo Channing." I pretended to smoke a cigarette. "Fasten your seat belts, it's going to be a bumpy night!"

"Nice," said my father. "But seriously, Lotus, he doesn't sound good, does he?"

"He'll be fine," I reassured my father. "I'll bring him some stuff from the Wellness Center tomorrow." I picked up a white pencil from the piles of makeup that were lying around and applied it as a highlighter under my eyes. My mother was also backstage, but she was not helping my father calm down. She kept waltzing in and asking me to get stuff for her.

"Are there any more comfortable chairs than this?"

"Do you really think that's the most flattering hairstyle on you, Lotus?"

"Why don't you come sit here with me, Lotus."

"I'm working, Maman. It's my *boulot,* my job."

I was trying not to worry, but when the dress rehearsal finally got going, it was a disaster. Man 2 kept forgetting his lines, Man 1 croaked all his lines, Man 3 messed up his blocking, and Man 4 added lines that hadn't been written. Not to mention how all the fake elliptical trainers fell over every two minutes and I had to keep putting them back together while Lorrie yelled at me the whole time to be careful. In the middle of Act 1, Man 2 was sitting on his elliptical trainer staring into space. I whispered his line to him: "I think today I'm really going to have a great workout."

He turned to me, totally going out of character. "If I wanted a line, young lady, I would have asked for one."

"Sorry, but—"

"No buts about it. Don't interrupt my artistic process again."

"Can we start from the top," said my father, wearily.

Almost everything went better this time. Man 2 remembered most of his lines, and the ones he didn't, I didn't tell him until he asked. But during Man 1's big fight about sweat with Man 3, Man 3 ignored his blocking and kept edging his way back onstage until Man 1 had to turn around and look at him. Then Man 1 went totally out of character and yelled hoarsely, "Just because I'm sick doesn't mean you have the right to upstage me."

Man 3 told him he was being paranoid, and then Man 4 got off his elliptical trainer to say something, but his machine fell over and there was a splitting sound that turned out to be his pants. Luke rushed onto the stage, swearing and smoking, and ordered Man 4 to take off the pants so he could fix them. I totally had to bite my lip to keep from laughing when Man 4 unzipped his pants and he had these big white boxers on underneath.

My father called a fifteen-minute break so Man 4 could get his pants fixed and Man 1 could get some hot tea. Sean and I sat outside on the steps and shared a Gauloise cigarette. I wanted to ask him about us, but I didn't want him to think I was being possessive. I also wanted to ask if he'd found my earring.

"I hope it's better tomorrow night," I said. "Because right

now it's kind of a mess. And that's the last time I help them with their stupid lines."

"Maybe I'll get to go on," said Sean, taking a drag on the cigarette.

"I think Man 1 will be okay. I'm going to bring him some elderberry extract."

"Being an understudy kind of sucks—having to want someone to get sick."

"I know what you mean. Hey, can I ask you something?"

"Sure."

"Well, it's just . . . now that our relationship is getting more *intime*, I mean, close, I know how important freedom is to you, but I just wanted to make sure that our relationship, you know, like J.P. and Simone's, is the primary one."

Sean took a long drag on the cigarette and looked at me. "What do you mean?"

"I thought you'd know this. Simone and J.P. both had what they called contingent relationships, like, with other people, because they were into total freedom, but they were still the most important people in the world to each other and they told each other everything."

Sean put his arm around me. "Well, you know you're important to me, Lotus, don't you?"

"Well, I guess, but after this afternoon . . ."

"This afternoon. Yeah, that was great, at least until we got interrupted. Could you believe that timing?"

"Yeah, that was awful, but I just need to know . . ."

Sean pulled me a little closer toward him. "Lotus, I don't know what to tell you. I am being honest with you, I just . . . I just don't think I'm ready to have a full-time

Simone de Beauvoir, if you know what I mean. But if I were, you would be the one."

I couldn't look at him because I was afraid if I did, I would start crying. "Oh."

He removed his arm and stubbed out his cigarette on the cement. "But we can still have fun, can't we?"

"*Bien sûr.*" I felt weird, like I needed to go outside and breathe some fresh air, even though I was outside already. I told Sean I had to go to Starbucks to get something for my mother and that I'd be back in *cinq* minutes.

I wandered over to Starbucks with Sean's words playing over and over in my head. The more I played them back, the worse they sounded.

When I got back, my father was sitting in the front row, moaning. "What was I thinking? Why did I ever quit my day job? I'm an idiot."

My mother came up to him and gently patted him on the shoulder. "Well, you know what they say about a bad dress rehearsal, honey."

"Yes, I do," said my father, turning to me. "It's a ridiculous theater superstition, Lotus, which claims that if you have a bad dress, you'll have a good opening night. I don't think it applies here, Suki."

My mother sighed. "Okay, okay, I was just trying to help."

I looked around for Sean. I saw him onstage, sitting on a fake elliptical trainer, studying his lines. I had felt so close to him yesterday, but now I felt so far away. Okay, he didn't want me to be his Simone de Beauvoir, but I was still important to him. I knew that. Fine. But who else was important to him? Joni? Portia? What did he really mean, anyway? At least Simone knew that J.P. thought she was the most important person in the world. Or did she? I started to think about Anne Frank again and was afraid I was going to cry. I walked back over to my father.

"Lotus, did you know we are having actual critics?" he said. "Real, newspaper-writing, sink-their-claws-into-you-pull-out-your-entrails critics, here tomorrow, in this very theater. I'm going to be a laughingstock."

"Dad, it's going to be fine." I said, "I'm sure of it. *Je suis sûre.*"

Adam showed up toward the end of the dress rehearsal with his drumsticks, which are now like his permanent accessory. He walked over to the side of the stage where I was standing with our mother.

"Don't you dare," said my mother, pointing at the drumsticks. "I still can't believe you gave up something you are so talented at to bang some sticks."

Adam rolled his eyes at me.

I tried to help. "You and Dad took us to hear that tribal drumming thing several times when we were little. That's probably where he got the idea."

My mother put her hands on her hips. "Lotus, Adam is not a tribesman and this isn't the time to discuss it, during your father's play. We're here to be supportive."

"You're the one who brought it up, Mom."

Adam twirled his drumsticks. "Mom, chess was for you. Drums are for me."

My mother started to plead with him, putting her hand

on his arm. "But you used to love to play. You begged us to let you skip dinner so you could do chess simulations on the computer."

"Yes, I enjoyed it when I was a kid. But for the past year, I've just been going through the motions."

My mother sighed.

My father came over and stood right in front of Adam. "Is that true, Adam?"

"That's what I've been trying to tell you."

In his *I'm the Dad* voice, my father turned to my mother. "Suki, if he wants to play drums, let him play drums. I've got a disaster of a play to fix." And then he exited left.

My mother picked up her decaf chai latte. She eyed it suspiciously. "Are you sure this is decaf, Lotus? Because it looks caffeinated."

"It's definitely decaf. I'm totally sure."

She took a long sip of the latte. "He'll regret it," she said.

"No, I won't," said Adam, hitting a drumstick on a wooden chair with a sharp crack.

"You will," said my mother.

"Well, that's my problem, isn't it?"

My mother stood there, drinking her latte, shaking her head slowly. "I'm done, Adam, I'm done trying. Do what you want. I've got too many other things to worry about. I've got a big outdoor benefit coming up and they're predicting rain and there's your father and the play and a million other things."

"Thanks, Mom." Adam went over and gave our mother a little squeeze around the waist. She spilled some of her latte, but seemed pleased at the physical contact. I looked at my watch and realized it was way past time for the second act to start.

"You people are not authorized to be back here," I said sternly. "Go sit in the audience."

Act 2 was a little better than Act 1, but everything still seemed off. I hoped what my mother said about dress rehearsals was true; otherwise, we were in trouble.

After the rehearsal was over, I picked up all the props and carefully put them away. The Unitarian church was having some Buddhist lovefest the next day and they'd go mental if everything was not in its place. It's always those love and peace people who have all the rules. By the time I was finished, I was sweaty and exhausted. Sean had left, and so had Adam and my mother.

I walked home with my father, who seemed less tense.

"I feel calmer now, Lotus, like everything is going to be okay."

"Maybe it's the Ativan."

"Well, I did take the other half Sean left in the dressing room, but I don't think that's it. I realize now that I'm going to fail, but it's okay."

"You're not going to fail, Dad. Your play is amazing."

"No, Lotus, I've written an entirely meaningless play about the meaninglessness of life. Props are falling over, actors are forgetting their lines, and the reviewers are going to tear it to shreds with their sharp little claws."

"Dad, that's so not true. Anyway, a lost battle is a battle one thinks one has lost."

"I guess you're right, Lotus. Who said that, Patton?"

"No, it was Jean-Paul Sartre, the *père* of modern existentialism."

"You're wise beyond your years, Lotus. Have I ever told you that?"

I walked closer to my father, his words seeping into me like something delicious and chocolaty. "Never. Usually, you tell me that I'm being ridiculous and juvenile."

nine

Vendredi, 15 Juin (Performance Day!!! Finally.)

This morning, I woke up and knew that I had found the perfect outfit to wear for the opening of *4 Men and Nothingness*, not to mention the cast party they were having afterward. It must have come to me in a dream, because the second I opened my eyes, I remembered a dress I had bought *très* long ago at a thrift store and then shoved in the back of my closet for a later date. It's sleeveless and black with a big white stripe going down the middle. My *grand-mère* said it was very Twiggy. "It's cute, but you're no Twiggy," added my mother when I came home and showed it to her. I knew it would look perfect with my mother's old platform sandals, which she has specifically forbidden me to wear because they have three-inch heels and she says that anything over an inch and a half will destroy my lumbar spine. But this morning I knew that if I wore this particular outfit, with a white band in my hair, everything would be perfect with the play, the critics, and Sean *et moi*.

One has to suffer for fashion, I told myself, as I crawled into the parental bedroom like a CIA operative. It was already nine o'clock, but my mother was still sleeping in her usual fetal position, her curvy cervical pillow under her neck. My father was at the other end of the bed, arms and legs sticking out. They were naked, but luckily *pour moi*, all their private parts were covered by the sheet—not that I'm a prude or anything, it's just that it would totally ick me out and probably traumatize me in some Freudian way. I crawled into the closet *de Maman* and scored the sandals. Safely back out in the hall, I picked a few splinters out of my hands and strapped the sandals on my feet. They looked wonderful with my white toenail polish.

At breakfast (such as it was: Clif Bars, absent parents, and pulpy orange juice), Adam asked if he could bring somebody to the play. I jotted down that he had a plus one on my list, which was getting really long, and took a Clif Bar for later, even though they taste like they are made of Elmer's glue and cardboard. I had so many things to remember, I needed an assistant. I needed to remember where the props went. And to deal with the cupcakes. And make the signs, and get change. And order drinks. And set up the coffee machine. I needed to remember to save seats for the people from the Wellness Center, my mom's boss, my *grand-mère*, and Ms. G, not to mention The Press. I had also invited a number of celebrities, who so far hadn't bothered to RSVP, which I think is *très* rude.

Celebrity List:

Christiane Amanpour (journaliste *par excellence, looks great in trench coat*)

Charlotte Gainsbourg (French pop star—not to mention actress—daughter of Serge, just put out new album)

Mireille Guiliano (FWDGF, of course, diet goddess)

Lauren Graham (formerly of Gilmore Girls, eats an enormous amount of food, never gains weight)

Julie Delpy (Sean's idea)

Johnny Depp (my idea)

After breakfast, I ran to the theater. Running is not so easy in platform sandals. Once, I almost tipped entirely to the left, but managed to right myself by flinging my weight to the right. I arrived at the Brooklyn Society for Ethical Culture exhausted. Helped set up the props. Helped with the run-through. Made coffee for Man 3, who said, "Lo, my angel of mercy, you are looking very fetching today," in that fake British scarf-tossed-around-the-neck way of his. I gave Man 1 little packets of herbs and detailed instructions from the Wellness Center. Man 3 tried to kiss my hand, but I pulled it away. Helped set up the chairs and attached Velcro to costumes for quick changes. Didn't even have time to eat my Clif Bar. Had the makeup *garçon* make me look like Marlo Thomas in *That Girl* with false eyelashes and pale lipstick. Ran into Sean, who did not kiss me hello, but did say, "Hey, like the dress."

The cupcakes arrived right on schedule, at four, *Dieu merci*. I paid the delivery guy with Joni's money, included a five-dollar tip, and got him to help me bring them into the hall to set them up. Excited, I opened the first box, but instead of HELL cupcakes staring back at me, there was a whole box of HELLO cupcakes. I ripped open the other box and saw that the OTHER and PEOPLE cupcakes were okay, but there was no IS cupcake, so instead of the whole sentence saying HELL IS OTHER PEOPLE, my cupcakes were going to say HELLO OTHER PEOPLE.

Merde, merde, and *double merde.*

I called Mrs. Maxwell's. Got the answering machine. Left angry message. "I don't know what kind of business you're running over there, but when I say I want HELL on a cupcake, I want HELL on a cupcake, not HELLO on a cupcake. I think I should get a refund, *tout de suite!* And for your information, I was not just cursing for cursing's sake, although I totally believe in free speech, I was quoting from a very famous, very intelligent man, Jean-Paul Sartre, the father of existentialism. I can't believe you've never heard HELL IS OTHER PEOPLE. And I have to tell you, Mrs. Maxwell, I'm really busy here and I don't need this agro, and I'm beginning to totally understand what J.P. meant by that sentence. Please call me back!"

I ran into my father in the hall. "Dad, you're not going to believe this—"

"Lotus, if the building is not on fire, I really can't deal with this right now."

"All right, all right, I'll handle it."

All the Men were pacing back and forth going over their lines, but I just ignored them and took a plastic knife and very carefully scraped off each O in HELLO. It took, like, hours and some of the cupcakes started to look a little smudged. So now I had HELL and OTHER PEOPLE, which was an improvement over HELLO OTHER PEOPLE. Then I took some of the HELLO cupcakes, which there seemed to be a lot of, and carefully scraped off the H and the E and the O and turned them sideways so I could make an equal sign out of the two Ls, making HELL = OTHER PEOPLE. That would have to do. Of course, after I had spent hours scraping every bit of icing off, who waltzed in but Joni, too late to help. It was so weird, seeing someone I was so close to come through the door like a stranger. I wanted to say something, but instead we just stood there in awkward silence, like people on a blind date.

Finally, I said, "Hey."

And she said, "Hey."

I looked at her more closely. She was wearing a short black skirt, which looked really good with her skinny legs. I had always bugged her to wear short skirts but she never would before.

"You look nice, Joni."

"So do you, Lotus."

"Yeah, I'm going for a whole Marlo Thomas *That Girl* kind of look." I remembered how we used to watch all those shows on the oldies television channel and how Joni wanted to be Mary Tyler Moore and I always wanted to be Marlo Thomas.

"Can I help with something?" Joni was looking at me as she said this, but not really looking at me.

"Sure." I smiled and tried to act like everything was fine between us. If it had been like the old days, I would have told her all about the HELL/HELLO cupcakes and we would have laughed about it. But as it was, I just couldn't muster up the enthusiasm to tell the story, so I just asked if she would man the cash register at intermission because she was better at math and if she could help set up the refreshments. I showed her where everything was, but she didn't seem to be paying attention and kept looking around for Sean and then pretending she wasn't.

"Sean's probably backstage, if you want to say hi," I told her.

Joni said, "Okay, thanks," as if she didn't care, but two minutes later, she asked me where the bathroom was and I knew she was going to look for Sean.

The hours before the play went by in a flash. By the time the curtain rose, I was exhausted. I had set up the cupcakes and the props, made coffee and got ice for iced coffee, helped with a sweat-suit wardrobe crisis and the last-minute prop check, found the exercise bands that were lost in the closet, arranged the programs, did a million other tasks for Lorrie the stage manager, and ignored Sean and Joni, who were acting all couply, fine, I don't care, *Je m'en fous*. Actually I did *fous* quite a lot, but I kept telling myself there was no time to melt down. But while we were setting up the refreshments together, I looked over at them and their hands were touching over some Diet Cokes and I couldn't stand to look at them. Was this how Joni felt, finding out about Sean and me kissing? It's one thing to know about something, but another to see them holding hands in front of you. I had to stop unpacking sodas and go into the supply closet to cry a little. But I couldn't stop crying and my mascara was already melting and I had way too much to do. I guess I did love Sean. Whenever I saw him, I felt *bouleversée*—that means swept off your feet—but I didn't have time right then to get emotional. I tried to imagine what all the people I admired would do in this situation.

Mme Guiliano: Definitely not eat. Perhaps sigh, have a glass of champagne, and wonder why Americans get so upset over infidelity, which is *totalement* natural and part of French life.

Sei Shōnagon: Be very dignified, contemplate a cherry blossom, maybe write a poem, pace around the courtyard, make a list of reasons why love sucks.

Simone de Beauvoir: Probably try to seduce Joni, but I'm not really ready for that. (Although it does seem very popular for girls to experiment with that, especially if they go to a college like Sarah Lawrence or Barnard.) Or else, she would put on really sturdy shoes and traipse around the woods for hours. There was no way I was buying those ugly hiking boots and going out into the wilderness by myself.

Just thinking about my heroes made me feel better. I wiped my face with a towel I found in the closet and emerged refreshed. When I got out of the closet, Sean was standing there, waiting for me. He pulled me back into the closet and started to kiss me and it felt amazing, like something I had been missing my entire life. I closed my eyes for a moment, but then I pulled back and looked at him.

"How did you know I was in here?"

"That makeup guy told me."

"Won't Joni be looking for you?"

"Come on, Lotus." He put his hand on my waist. "Don't be mad. Come here. Look, I know this looks . . . really bad. But the thing is, Lotus, I really do like you, but I really like Joni, too, and with all she's been going through with her mom she needs me more than you do."

"What are you talking about? What's she been going though?"

"You don't know?" He took a step back.

"No."

"She had a breakdown." Sean looked so TV-movie-of-the-week serious while he was telling me this, I couldn't understand what he was saying.

"Joni?"

"No, her mom."

"Oh my God! Julia? That's unbelievable." I was stunned. Joni's mom had been so sick, and I hadn't even known about it.

"She's okay now, but she's kind of out of it, you know—medicated in a major way."

"What happened?"

"I don't know exactly, but Joni said she just started cleaning all the time, much more than usual. And buying supplies. Like bleach and ammonia and those Bounce dryer sheets. They were stacked up everywhere. It was like a giant storeroom. And she wouldn't sleep. In the middle of the night, she was scrubbing the tub so much her hands were bleeding."

Sean put his arm around me. "She had to go into the hospital, but only for a few days. Then they released her."

"I can't believe I didn't know about this. . . . I could have . . . I don't know . . . done something."

"You couldn't have done anything," said Sean, kissing my neck, softly, gently.

It still felt great, but it also felt wrong. I had a sudden, strange urge to see my mother, see if she was okay.

I pulled away. "I've got to go."

I went back and helped Joni with the rest of the drinks. While we were doing the refreshments, I kept looking at Joni and trying to tell what she was feeling, but I couldn't get anything from her face. She was smiling, laughing, chatting with everyone who walked by. When Sean came back, she looked so happy. I had an urge to go over and touch her arm or something, but there was this huge cold front between us, this iceberg of separation. I didn't want to ruin her good time, although I wished she was having it with anyone but Sean.

The audience started arriving, so I had to pull it together and be all upbeat. I was smiling so much, I felt like I was at a beauty pageant, but all I could really think about was Joni and her mom, and Sean kissing me, and how nothing happened for so long in my life and then everything happened at once.

My *grand-mère* came in with her date, a gray-haired guy named Chuck who was wearing one of those awful baggy multicolored sweaters.

He shook my hand. "You must be Lotus Flower."

"It's just Lotus, but nice to meet you."

My *grand-mère* told me Chuck had a boat, and he invited me to go out on it with them. I told him that I got seasick, but he said that he had these Japanese wrist straps that activated acupressure points. Everyone from the Wellness Center walked in then, so I took them all to their seats and handed out programs.

The play, *incroyablement*, went great. In Act 1, every Man remembered his lines and his blocking, and there was no serious upstaging. I stood in the wings, but all I did was watch, mouthing some of the parts to myself. I almost gave a line once, but then I realized that Man 2 was doing one of his dramatic pauses, so I just stayed quiet. The most amazing part of the whole thing was that the audience loved it. My *grand-mère* always says that if there isn't much coughing during a play, it's a success. There was hardly any coughing. They laughed in *beaucoup de* places and clapped like crazy at the end of the first act. I was thrilled for my father, but as I watched Sean and Joni across the wings, sitting so close together (he had snuck her backstage), I felt lonely.

Intermission was a zoo. The cupcakes and the raffle were a huge hit. Joni and Sean were both helping, seeming like the perfect couple. People kept buying the HELL, mostly because saying "I want a Hell" is so much more fun than saying "I want an Other" or "I want a People."

My brother came over to the table and grabbed a cupcake. "That'll be two fifty," I said, snatching it out of his hand.

"No *problemo*, give me another HELL."

I noticed the girl by his side, cute, with a short plaid skirt and a big white men's shirt. I elbowed my brother until he said, "Lotus, this is Satchiko."

"*Enchantée*. My brother's told me *absolument rien* about you."

Satchiko told me she met my brother at a chess match (she doesn't play anymore) and that she was a drummer in a band.

"Kind of like Lane from *Gilmore Girls*," I said.

She shrugged. "I don't know. My parents don't let me watch television."

"I totally sympathize—our parents make us drink soy milk instead of regular milk, and I don't even have a cell phone."

Act 2 went great, except for an incident where a bicycle fell over during Man 3's monologue about heart rate monitors. Everyone laughed like crazy, so it was okay. At the end of the play, when everyone came out and took their bows, I felt so proud, like I had done all the acting, writing, and directing myself. At the end of all the clapping and the encores, they started crying, "Author, author," and my father came out and took a bow and everyone clapped.

Two seconds later, when I saw him in the wings, he was shaking his head and whispering something about cretins.

"Dad, what's up? They loved it—you should be so excited."

"Lotus, didn't you hear them? They were laughing. Laughing like idiots. My play isn't a comedy. It's a serious commentary on the meaninglessness of our consumer culture."

"But Dad, they only laughed at certain things. Not everything. Anyway, if they laughed, you should take it as a compliment. Think of all those poor sitcom writers who can't get anyone to laugh at their lame jokes."

"I guess." He was still pacing and shaking his head.

"They liked it. That's the important thing—they liked your play. Yours. And you know, Dad, that bicycle thing was funny."

"I suppose." He smiled, kind of reluctantly.

"You should go out there and talk to *la presse*. Don't tell them you wanted it to be serious. Just act mysterious."

"Okay, I'll be out in a minute."

Out in the hall, everyone was chatting and getting ready to go to the party, which was going to be upstairs in the same building. Joni and Sean had wandered off, after a half-hearted offer to clean up. I told them I was fine. But I wasn't. I didn't even know how I felt. I kept thinking about Sean, Sean and me, Sean and Joni, and most of all, Joni's mom. I thought about how it must have been for Joni, seeing her mom unravel like that, and how I hadn't been there for her.

For the cast party, the Men had ordered pizza from Two Boots and my father bought a case of prosecco, which they were mixing with different juices. I got there late, after the pizza was cold, because me and Lorrie stayed to put everything away. I tried to send positive vibrations to Joni, but I don't think she received them, because she didn't even look at me. I also practiced not looking at Sean, not thinking about Sean, and not having anything to do with Sean. It wasn't going very well, because I kept looking at him and thinking about him.

I introduced Ms. G to Man 1. She was looking good in a print skirt and a black sweater and what looked like a bit of lip gloss. They both stood there, totally silent, so I had to start the conversation for them. "What did you think of the play?" I asked Ms. G. She started saying softly how she admired his performance and how she could never do that, and then he said, "But you *do* perform—you're a teacher," and she smiled. A few minutes later, I overheard him telling her all about his book club. All was well in Fix-up Land.

Everyone was drinking champagne and talking about how great and funny the play was. I could see that my father had gotten over thinking funny was bad. In fact, he was acting like he had planned each and every joke, even the bicycle falling over, which was a total accident. All the actors were running around and hugging and kissing, as if they were all best friends.

"So, what did you think of my performance?" asked Man 3, grabbing my arm as I walked past.

"It was great."

He began telling me about every time he had gotten a laugh and analyzing why some lines didn't get a laugh, and I tried to look really interested, in case Joni or Sean looked over, but when I looked over at them, they were only looking at each other. My father was chatting up a reviewer from the *Park Slope Reader*. Ms. G was talking to Man 1. My *grand-mère* and Chuck were holding hands. My brother and Satchiko were throwing pepperoni at each other. The people from the Wellness Center were having a heated discussion about magnet therapy. Even my mom looked happy. It was like everyone had someone but me.

"How old are you, anyway?" asked Man 3, pausing in his boring discussion of acting techniques. "I don't want to get in trouble."

I took a sip of his champagne. "Age is irrelevant, don't you think? Tell me more about Stella Adler."

A little later, I ran into Joni at the makeshift bar.

The bartender, a friend of my father's, was lining up plastic champagne glasses. "So, ladies, what will you be having: soda, sparkling water, juice?"

Joni and I giggled involuntarily at his calling us ladies.

"I'll have some champagne," I said.

"You two lovelies are not by any chance underage, are you?"

"You know, if we were in France," I told him, "we would have been drinking wine practically since we could talk. *C'est vrai*."

Joni nodded. "It's true."

"Okay," he said, looking around to see if anyone was watching. "Just this once."

He poured a splash of black currant juice into two champagne glasses and then filled them with prosecco. "Here you go. Two of our special existential cocktails. One Simone de Beauvoir and one Jean-Paul Sartre."

"But they're exactly the same drink," said Joni.

"Or are they?" quipped the bartender.

Joni and I clinked our plastic glasses silently, but our momentary bond was already disintegrating. She had stopped smiling and was looking around again, probably for Sean. I tried to get the mood back.

"Joni, I just wanted to tell you that I'm really sorry about your mom being sick. I wish I had known."

Joni's voice came out sounding weird and harsh. "Why? You couldn't have stopped it."

"Yeah, but—"

"It's okay," Joni said, biting her lip. "She had a manic episode, but it's no big deal. She's on medication now—it's a chemical thing, she's not crazy or anything."

"I know she isn't."

Sean came up and interrupted us. It was the first time I wasn't happy to see him. Joni smiled and held her glass to his lips and he took a sip. I headed toward the food table. I had two slices of cold pizza and started chatting to Man 2, who, if you kind of scrunched your eyes, looked like Johnny Depp. I almost wished I could develop a crush on him, but as Mrs. Who says in *A Wrinkle in Time*, *Le coeur a ses raisons que la raison ne connaît point*, which loosely translates as "you can't choose whom you have a crush on."

Man 4, the older guy I had once thought would be good for my *grand-mère*, was chatting to her by the cookie tray. Out of the corner of my eye, I saw Chuck heading over to the cookies. Maybe they would have a duel over my *grand-mère*, Chuck in his multicolored sweater and Man 4 in his polo shirt.

After an hour or so, Ms. G came over to say goodbye.

"You're wearing lip gloss, aren't you?" I asked her, feeling proud.

She looked embarrassed. "A little."

"It's not a crime. What about the rest of the makeup we got?"

"I have to start small, I guess. I'll get to it."

"Try the eyeliner next time. It makes a huge difference," I suggested.

"So, Lotus, I haven't gotten any notice about the next meeting of the French club. We still need to do a lot of planning for Montreal."

I looked over at Joni and Sean, huddled in a corner. "I don't even know if I want to go anymore."

Ms. G followed my gaze. "Oh. I see."

"Yeah." It was weird, like we were having a whole conversation about Joni and Sean without saying anything.

"Lotus, you shouldn't let anything spoil this for you. It's a great opportunity."

"*Peut-être.* Maybe."

"Promise me you won't decide anything till the next meeting, okay?"

"Okay."

Man 1 came over to Ms. G and she smiled shyly.

The bartender had disappeared, so I grabbed a half-empty bottle of prosecco and headed outside. I sat on the back stoop of the Society for Ethical Culture, not caring how dirty it was, not caring how many filthy shoes had stepped where my butt now was. I drank my prosecco, but I couldn't taste it—it could have been anything. There was a chocolate smudge on the front of my dress and I didn't even care. It was all so meaningless. Everything ended. The play. Me and Sean. Me and Joni. Life. Why even begin anything? Why bother? I drank more prosecco. I could sit out here for days, until they found my lifeless, malnourished body being nibbled on by dogs and no one would even care.

I tried to get up, but everything decided to move with me—the sidewalk, the stairs, my stomach. After a few minutes, I tried again and got up and started walking home, fast. No one was home when I got there but *Pierre le chien,* who looked at me like he knew exactly what I was going through. I gave him some soy kibble, drank a large glass of water, and lay diagonally across my bedspread, watching the room spin.

In the moment before I lost consciousness, I thought, *This is it, this is exactly what Jean-Paul Sartre was talking about in* La Nausée. It's not just a physical feeling; it's a nausea with everything: everything around you, the lameness of your whole life. I still felt dizzy and sick, but the thought of sharing those nauseous feelings with J.P. was strangely comforting.

Lundi, Mardi, Mercredi, whatever.

Time passed. Slowly. Very slowly. Everyone in the world was happy but me.

I should have been happy. School was over for the year and I had done pretty well in all my classes. Ms. G had given me an A for my diary project, which she said was very original, and I even got a B+ in French, thanks to all the extra credit I got for starting a French club. But I didn't feel happy. I just felt nothing.

Jeudi, 21 Juin

I woke up and remembered what day it was. It was my birthday, except it didn't feel like my birthday because ever since I can remember, Joni and I have celebrated our birthdays with each other. She always takes me out for lunch—usually macaroni and cheese and chocolate cake—and then gives me earrings and a scratch-off lottery ticket for each year I've been alive. Then, for dinner, my parents order whatever I want and we have more chocolate cake and I get some lame presents.

It's so bizarre not being friends with Joni anymore. What happened to our friendship anyway? It felt so real for all those years and then in a flash, poof, it was gone. Are some other girls enjoying our friendship in some other borough of New York, or in Hong Kong, or on another planet? If our friendship can go wrong, then anything can happen—like all the things Joni's mom worries about: bird flu, the plague, alien invasion. They could all come true.

I was so stupid. I can't believe that I thought for a millisecond that Joni and I could both like Sean and it would end up okay. It was *ridicule*. When I saw them together at the play, it really hurt, and I finally understood what Joni must have felt when I told her that Sean had kissed me, and I feel horrible about it.

So this year, another birthday, but no Joni. It's fine, birthdays are ridiculous and juvenile anyway. Why should I celebrate that I am one year—actually, one day—older than yesterday and that much closer to death? I wasn't angry or anything, but I think it would have been nice if Joni had risen above our petty differences to send me a card even if she didn't want to talk to me.

I couldn't help but wonder if the *famille* was going to do anything special for me, but no, when I arrived in the kitchen for breakfast, there were no festivities, just me alone with some Uncle Sam cereal and black coffee because my mother forgot to go shopping again. It's not surprising. *Mes parents* have been very self-involved lately. My father is always off writing now and my mother is working on some ADD benefit, so she's always rushing off to meetings. Since he got his playwriting grant, my *père* says the house is too quiet for any real creativity, so he rented a cubicle in a playwright's community where he writes all day long, except for long periods chatting in the coffee room. Apparently, there's quite a rivalry over who makes the best French press coffee in the Brooklyn Writers Nook. "It's all part of the process," he tells me. Even coffee making.

Mes parents have been disgustingly happy lately, practically making out at dinner until my brother and I start coughing and then they laugh and stop. Apparently playwriting grants are a great aphrodisiac. I checked my e-mail, just to see if anyone remembered my *anniversaire*. Nothing from Joni. I wasn't disappointed or anything, it just felt odd. And Sean, of course, doesn't even know when my birthday is, which is fine, because my feelings for him are ancient history. I just wish I could have kissed someone else since that night at the play, so I could stop thinking about him.

Scrolling through all the junk e-mail and an e–birthday card from my *grand-mère*, I saw a gazillion e-mails from Ms. G, which I was sure were about the trip to Montreal. I didn't have the heart to tell her I wasn't going. I didn't even click on her e-mails, I just left them sitting there looking sad and unopened.

Correspondence is futile anyway.

I still had the money from the existential cupcake sale in my old Miss Piggy piggy bank. I haven't even counted it, much less figured out what to do with it. I used to be so broke, but in the past couple of weeks, I've paid off all the money I owed my brother and my mother with my checks from the Wellness Center. I've even saved a little. You know life is grim when you don't feel like shopping and you're saving money out of boredom.

Went to work on my birthday wearing an old Gap T-shirt and jeans and with dirty hair.

Barbara was shocked. "Is that you, Lotus? I hardly recognized you. You're so casual."

"It's me. *C'est moi. Après moi, le déluge,* as they say."

"Who says?"

"Louis the fifteenth of France. It means 'After me, the flood.' "

Sheila tried to take my temperature, but I said I was fine. Later, Barbara had the Reiki master wave his bony hands over my entire body to see what was wrong with me. Apparently the energy in my third chakra is very blocked and my aura is muddled. Great.

After work, I went to the Botanic Garden and lay on the grass. I thought about how Sean and I used to go there. I felt a dull ache in my chest, but I wasn't entirely sure if it was heartburn from the burrito I ate at lunch, the blockage in my third chakra, or actual heartbreak. While I was trying to figure this out, a guard came over and told me I couldn't lie on my giant blue ELLE beach towel because it would flatten the grass.

"More than my entire body lying on the grass?" I argued. "That makes no sense."

He shrugged. "Hey, don't blame me, I don't make the rules."

"I didn't realize this was a gulag," I muttered as he walked away.

As soon as he was gone, I lay down on my towel again. I felt a little better by disobeying the guard and ate some forbidden onion-and-sour-cream potato chips. I have totally stopped my healthy French way of eating and am back to my old habits. *Au revoir* croissants, *bonjour* junk food. I lay there looking up at the sky. The air was hot and sticky, but the trees were totally shading me from the sun with a green canopy of leaves. I told myself positive things.

It's okay to be alone.

I don't need anyone.

Birthdays are meaningless bourgeois rituals.

I think I must have fallen asleep, because the guard came over to tell me the garden was closing and I had to leave. On the way home, I stopped at Joyce Bakeshop and got a lemon bar and a cappuccino. Happy birthday to me!

Went home. No mention of what day it was by my mother, my father, or my brother. Everything disgustingly normal. Went to my room and lay down on my bed until dinner. After dinner (grilled tilapia, edamame, and brown rice), my mother carried in a big chocolate cake, lit with sixteen tiny candles, and they all started singing. *Happy birthday to you, Happy birthday, dear Lotus, Happy birthday to you!!!*

"I bet you thought I forgot, Lotus," said my mother, smiling widely. "Actually, I did, but then I remembered."

"Make a wish," said Adam, nudging me.

"That's okay," I said, blowing out my candles and wishing my mother was Christiane Amanpour.

"Hey, Mom, what's that weird flavor?" asked Adam, taking a cautious bite of the cake.

"It's carob, honey."

"It is supposed to be chocolate," I said. "I always have chocolate cake on my birthday."

"Oh, Lotus, you can't tell the difference," said my mother, cutting me an enormous lopsided slice.

"It's delicious, Suki," said my father, giving her a slap on the butt.

Adam and I looked at each other and rolled our eyes. Because of my newfound indifference to life, I went along with the idea that the cake was edible. My father told us all about his new play, something about aliens and quantum physics that is called *Quarks in Love*. He got up and waved his arms around. "It's a whole new kind of physical theater melding quantum physics and philosophy."

My mother stared at him, starry-eyed. "And a love story?" she asked hopefully.

"Yes, that too," said my father, his mouth full of cake.

We ate the weird cake (which tasted somewhat better with whipped cream) and I even got a present I liked for once: an iPod Nano.

Adam said, "Welcome to the modern world, sis," and hit me on the arm.

I grabbed his hand. "If you hit me one more time, you won't live to your next birthday."

My parents were looking so pleased with themselves, I tried to work up some enthusiasm despite my underlying depression. "*C'est super chouette.* That means 'super great'. Thanks, guys." I gave my mother and father a hug and for a moment felt almost happy. Adam gave me a gift certificate to iTunes and promised he would set up my Nano on the family computer for me. It wasn't a perfect birthday, but it was better than I had expected.

That night, I had insomnia for a really long time and thought about my future. Maybe I'd become one of those women who stayed with their parents forever. I'd be eccentric and get square red eyeglasses and take up some obscure sport, like fencing or snooker, and spend all my free time talking about it in chat rooms and playing Second Life. I'd get really into cleaning and knitting and wear spinster clothes, which are very similar to hipster clothes but worn less layered by someone much older. My parents would tell everyone, "We don't know how we'd manage without our Lotus," but feel sorry for me because I was so pathetic and didn't have a life of my own.

Vendredi, 22 Juin

"Happy day after your birthday, Lotus. Do you want some Egg Beaters and turkey bacon?"

I sighed. "Mom, you do know that the yolk contains all the vital nutrients of the egg?"

"You can't even taste the difference, Lotus."

"You keep saying that, but I always taste the difference."

"Just try it."

I choked down some anemic-looking Egg Beaters with the addition of buttered toast, jam, and artisanal sheep's milk Camembert.

"So, Lotus, I got a call from Ms. G about your trip to Montreal."

Oh my God. Montreal. I had to make this go away. There was no way I could sit there and watch Joni and Sean together. I couldn't even bear to think about it.

"Mom, listen, before you say anything else. I've been doing a lot of thinking about this whole Montreal trip, and I don't think that it's a good time for me. I've got a lot of things going on right now, and anyway, I think I'm going to save my money and go to Paris after I graduate."

"Well, Lotus, I just think you shouldn't make any rash decisions."

"Mom, I'm not going. No matter how many faux breakfasts you make. Not even if you start wearing an apron."

My mother strapped on some bizarre-looking sneakers with uneven thick soles.

"Freaky sneaks, Mom."

"Do you like them? They're called MBTs. They're modeled on the walking habits of the Masai tribe. You burn twice as many calories because you're slightly off balance." She stood up and started to tip over, so I pushed her upright.

"Thanks. Look, I'm late for my Walkilates—we'll talk about this later."

"Nothing to talk about. Bye. And be careful."

She walked precariously out the front door. It was so hot I couldn't stand it. *Mes parents* don't believe in air-conditioning unless the weather report shows the scary red-thermometer heat advisory, so after I walked *Pierre le chien* slowly around the block, I just lay around the house listening to podcasts, sweating, and eating Popsicles. Since my birthday, I've become attached to a woman named Leticia who does a podcast called "One Thing in a French Day."

I listen to it to practice my French accent. Already, I've learned random factoids like the French are the *plus râleur* (grumpiest) workers in the world, that French women take special herbs to help them breast-feed (ick), that François Mitterrand had a mistress and no one in France cared (interesting), and that they eat something called *cerfeuille*. I'm not sure what it is, but you can make it into a soup with ravioli. If I ever had a kid, which is pretty doubtful, I would definitely have it in France because they have government-run day care in each neighborhood (they call it a crash) where you can dump your kid for two days a week for free.

I imagined myself in France, kind of like Leticia but without the baby and the husband, just me living near Paris with a cute accent and a podcast. I would meet Leticia on the days when she dropped the baby off at the crash and we would go have the most delicious coffee and pastries and eat soup made with *cerfeuille*.

In the afternoon, my *grand-mère* and I went for our annual special birthday excursion. She said we needed to do something I had never done before, so we went to Belmont to see the horse races. I met her at the Long Island Rail Road station and we took the train, played cards, and ate the little chocolate candies she brought.

Once we got there we went straight to the clubhouse, not the stands, which was just as well because the people in the regular part were kind of depressing, mostly a lot of slouchy men who looked sad. All in all, the races were not what I expected. I thought there would be a lot of people in wide-brimmed hats with billowy white clothes, but instead there were a lot of short grubby men with baseball caps. Luckily, we had a reservation at the restaurant, so we didn't have to hang out with them.

Each table had its own miniature TV screen so you could do all your betting without ever getting up and going to the window. You could also look down through the giant picture windows and see the actual horses. I showed my *grand-mère* how to use the betting screen, but at the end of the day she confessed she liked the old-fashioned way of betting better.

We both ordered shrimp cocktail and Caesar salad and she gave me forty dollars to bet with. I bet strictly by name of the horse, but my *grand-mère* had a very complicated handicapping system involving the maternal line of the horse, the jockey, and the condition of the track. I told her all about how I didn't want to go to Montreal because of Joni and Sean, and how my mother wanted to talk me into it.

"I'm sure your mother thinks you'll get something out of it."

"She has no idea what I'm going through."

"Lotus, honey, I totally understand why you don't want to go to Montreal—a broken friendship is a terrible thing. Did I ever tell you about my friend Dottie? Well, it was all a misunderstanding over a boy, but we didn't speak for ten years and it was a terrible shame."

"Joni hates me."

"She doesn't hate you. She's just holding a grudge and she doesn't know how to let it go. A grudge can be very comforting when things are falling apart all around you."

I doodled on my racing form. "I don't care about her and Sean, or what they do together, but I don't think I can take spending four days with them slobbering all over each other."

"Lotus, I think you could do much better than that boy. He's charming and he's certainly attractive, but there are other qualities that are better for the long run."

"I don't know. I think that's it for me in the *amour* department. Speaking of *l'amour*, how's Chuck?"

"Well, at this point in my life, Lotus, I have low expectations, so we get along fine. Dinner twice a week and bridge on Sundays. It's perfect. I don't cook for him, I don't clean for him, and we sleep in our own beds."

"I hear you. After Sean, my expectations of men are worse than low, they're nonexistent."

"Don't say that. It's like the races, honey bun, if you don't bet, you can't win."

"Right. Back to business." I entered our PIN on our private betting screen. "I'm betting on Heretic, Damsel in Distress, and Tally's Fever in the fourth race, for the trifecta."

"Hmmm. Trifectas are tricky. Make sure to box it, so you can win either way. And put ten dollars on Elsa's Future to win for me, okay? Edgar Prado's a great jockey and she does well on the turf."

For a moment I started having an alternate view of my future, involving OTB, scotch sours, and Gamblers Anonymous. After lunch, we had ice cream sundaes. Between races, I went to the window where you could look at the horses as they came down to exercise. My *grand-mère* had already won two hundred dollars and I had lost my forty. Lesson of the day: Trifectas are sucker bets. Winners bet to win.

As we stood at the opening of the paddock, one horse walked right over to me and I petted its nose. It wasn't one of the racehorses, it was one of the horses that accompany the racehorses down to the track so they don't feel alone.

I stroked the horse's nose while the handler stared at me, incredulous. "That horse, she doesn't let anyone touch her. You must have the magic," he said. His voice, with its soft Irish accent, was hypnotic. "You, young lady, have the touch. You are the chosen one. You pulled the sword from the stone." I felt so happy then, as if everything was going to magically fall into place.

On the train ride home, I kept repeating to myself, *You pulled the sword from the stone*, which I knew was from *The Once and Future King*, which is all about King Arthur and Lancelot and Guinevere. I've read it like three times.

Samedi, 23 Juin

In the morning, my mother asked if I needed to go shopping.

"You know, for Montreal," she added, putting mangos and soy yogurt and some other stuff in the blender to make a smoothie.

"Mom!"

"Hold on, Lotus." She pushed the button and an enormous grinding noise ensued.

I waited an eternity, my hands over my ears, until the horrible noise stopped and then watched in horror as my mother poured a strange-looking green mixture into a martini glass.

"That color is so wrong, Mom. Why is it green?"

"Oh, it's the wheatgrass juice. You want some?"

"Not in this lifetime. Thanks, though."

"So, about Montreal."

"I told you, I'm not going."

"Lotus, what are you talking about? It's all arranged. I just got off the phone with Ms. G, and you and your friends are going a week from Tuesday. We can't make any changes, because your father and I are going to the Omega Center— there's an amazing goddess program there."

I thought I had misheard her. "Dad's going to a goddess weekend at the Omega Center? Get out of here!"

"Don't be ridiculous, Lotus. It's for women only. He's going to be attending a creativity seminar while I'm at the goddess convention, but we're going to meet up at a couples drumming workshop on Saturday night."

My mother was in multitask mode now, dumping food in Pierre's bowl, rinsing out her blender full of disgusting green gook, and stuffing papers into her briefcase.

"I bet. Hey, Mom, can you listen to me for a moment? Please put down the papers and try to focus. I'm not going to Montreal. It's not going to happen. And anyway, what about Joni? Her mother's been sick, so she'll definitely want to be there for her. There's no way she'll go."

"Lotus, Joni is a teenager, not a psychiatrist. And for the record, Joni's mom is doing much better. In fact, Joni's parents are going to take this opportunity and go on a cruise to the Greek Isles to do some bonding of their own, so it works out for everyone. You may not realize this, but it's not easy taking care of a teenager. And your father and I have already sent our nonrefundable deposit to the Omega Center, so that's that."

"So, I'm just chattel, is that it? You just send me wherever you want, like a package, and don't care about what *I* want?"

"*Chattel* is a good SAT word, Lotus honey, make a note of it." My mother sighed and paced around the stove. "I really don't understand you, Lotus. Two weeks ago, you were dying to go, and now you're acting like I'm torturing you by making it happen."

"It's just . . . it's complicated. . . . Mom, do you know you have a weird green mustache?"

My mom wiped her mouth with a paper towel. "Look, Lotus, I wasn't going to bring this up, but your father told me about your cute friend Sean and how he's been spending time with Joni, and I just don't think you should miss out on this trip because of some teenage jealousy."

"Mom, listen, it's not . . . I don't . . . How does Dad know anyway?"

"You know actors, they're all terrible gossips. Look, Lotus, I've really got to go. I have an important meeting." She gulped the rest of the green mixture down and grabbed her laptop. "We'll talk."

ten

Lundi, 25 Juin

I have refused to go to Montreal. Refused to shop. Refused to pack. I am going to stay in my room and eat instant macaroni and cheese and reread The Lord of the Rings and His Dark Materials until the End of Days.

Jeudi, 28 Juin

I am slowly starting to get sick of macaroni and cheese and a little excited about going to Montreal. I haven't talked to Sean or Joni, but Ms. G keeps sending me e-mails with the weather forecast in Montreal. I've even started to pack.

Mardi, 3 Juillet

What can I say? *J'adore Montréal.* Well, that is, I'm sure I will adore Montreal once I actually get there, but for now I am still trapped on this interminable journey. At least I'm able to listen to my French podcasts in peace. Joni and Sean are sitting in an entirely different car than Ms. G and me, so the other good news is that I don't have to watch them making out for ten hours. It's like we're all going on different trips. Joni is wearing khaki cargo pants and carrying her mother's Louis Vuitton luggage, as if she were going hiking in Saint-Tropez. I brought an antique hatbox and a small duffel bag of my brother's, which I'm not crazy about but it holds a lot of stuff. Sean just has a backpack because all he ever wears is the same pair of faded jeans and weird band T-shirts. Today he is wearing one that says Monster Bobby. Ms. G brought a medium-sized wheelie bag and very sensible sandals. I have my work cut out for me there.

Emotions when I saw Sean and Joni, being all togetherish:
Jealousy (I guess my mother was right and I'm not really over it)
Annoyance (all happy couples inspire annoyance because they make you feel inadequate and like you're a voyeur)
Happiness (strangely, I feel happy for Joni that she's found someone)

I love looking out the window of the train, watching the United States get farther and farther away, but Amtrak does have a lot to answer for: The snacks are atrocious, quite expensive, and entirely American, even though we are heading for French Canada. For example, what the hell is a Santa Fe chicken sandwich doing on a train to Montreal? I plan to write a letter to the president of Amtrak to explain that a croissant sandwich is an entirely different creature than a real croissant and perhaps should be illegal!

When I first got on the train it seemed kind of glamorous, like the Orient-Express, but after four and a half hours and using a train bathroom several times, I am ready for the trip to be over.

Here's what I've done so far:

Heure 1

Listened to the Weepies (one of my new favorite bands) on my Nano and obsessed about the fact that I packed the wrong things. I based all packing on an article I read on a fashionista blog that involved famous models' packing techniques. The one I chose involved bringing very light, stretchy clothes in two colors (I picked black and purple). For a moment, I thought that maybe I should have brought some cargo pants with pockets, like Joni is wearing. On second thought, *non*, because they make even Joni's butt look big. Or a dark blue jean jacket, like Sean is wearing, for when it is super air-conditioned, like now. But then I remembered how I hate jean jackets—they are too bulky and the pockets are weirdly placed over your boobs. I was freezing, so I started digging around in my bag, ruining my careful, neat packing in the process. I finally found a stretchy lilac sweater, which was perfect.

While I was packing, my mother kept saying things like "Lotus, I really think you should bring a sturdy pair of walking shoes," or "Lotus, how about a nice Unitarian sweatshirt, in case it gets cold." She even wanted me to bring shorts! *Quelle horreur.*

Heure 2

Went to train bathroom. Should have held it in for ten hours and forty-five minutes because the bathroon smelled and I couldn't get the heavy door to lock and it kept opening and each time it started sliding open I had to fling myself from my seated position on the toilet to the door so no one would see me. Had *très* embarrassing close call with a train conductor with handlebar mustache because he started to open the door before I got to it, but I don't think he saw all that much (or at least that's what I choose to believe).

T-shirts I noticed on train:

(on chubby dark-haired girl in *très* short skirt) FUTURE TROPHY WIFE

(on tall skinny kid with acne) WHY COULDN'T I HAVE BEEN BORN RICH INSTEAD OF HANDSOME

Question: Why do Americans who travel to other countries insist on making the worst possible impression?

Heure 3

Tried talking to Ms. G, but she wanted to read her book. It's called *Suite Française* and she said it was very engrossing. I like the title, but I think it is something depressing about the Holocaust. I asked to borrow it after she was finished. I brought *The Decameron* to read, because I love books about the plague, but I can't read on a train because I get nauseated.

Heure 4

Went to the café. Had terrible Amtrak coffee and burned my tongue. I should sue and retire with millions of dollars. I am going to write a guide to where to get decent coffee all over the world, although I'm afraid it would be more of a pamphlet. Sat in the lounge, which is just a bunch of plastic tables filled with parents and sullen children reading Harry Potter (*quel cliché*) and a bunch of old people, some of whom are playing games like bridge or working on their computers or texting each other endlessly. Sat down and successfully avoided chitchat with other passengers by putting on my headphones and listening to the latest Charlotte Gainsbourg CD. Charlotte G is very skinny and always looks like she just did heroin (not that I know what that looks like from personal experience, but I have watched a lot of Lifetime television).

Heure 5

Went to the café (again) out of boredom. Joni was two people behind me in line, but we ignored each other as the line inched forward *incroyablement* slowly. When I got to the front and the Amtrak guy asked me what I wanted, I pointed to the one remaining fruit and cheese plate. Behind me, Joni sighed loudly.

I turned around. "Hey, what's your problem?"

"I was going to get that," she muttered, still not looking at me.

I was shocked. I know how much Joni hates confrontation and here she was all up in my face. Once, she let a popular girl in fourth grade steal her favorite pink coat because she was too shy to confront her about it, even though it was obvious the girl knew it wasn't hers, and then she was stuck with the girl's inferior pink coat for the rest of the winter.

Instinctively, I moved my hand to hover over the Camembert on the cheese and fruit plate to show that it was mine. At the same moment, Joni walked forward and put her hand over the cracker side of the shrink-wrapped plastic tray. The people who were between us stepped aside silently, as if we were in the Wild West and about to have a shoot-out.

"It's my cheese plate," I said loudly. I felt strange and powerful and angry.

Joni tried to appeal to the Amtrak guy in his red jacket, saying that she had gluten allergies and couldn't eat bread and that was why she needed the cheese plate.

I turned to her. "You don't have gluten allergies. You're making it up."

"You don't know everything about me." She turned to the other people on line, as if to convince them. "I'm a very honest person, *unlike some people*. I can't believe you think I'm making it up."

"What I think is that you are a person who is not getting a cheese plate, so why don't you just go back to your boyfriend and leave me alone."

"You know, not everything belongs to you, Lotus."

"Look, Joni, I don't know what your problem is, but right now we are under Amtrak international train laws, and therefore whoever saw it first, gets it."

Joni glared at me. "You've probably eaten two cheese plates already."

"Joni, did anyone ever tell you you're a bitch?" I wanted to slap her or pour coffee on her clean white T-shirt.

"Takes one to know one."

"Ladies, ladies, break it up," said the Amtrak café guy, in an amused but firm way. "There's one cheese plate and this young lady has dibs on it." He put it in front of me. "But we have plenty of other items of interest for the other young lady. How about a nice Santa Fe sandwich or a hot dog?"

I paid for my cheese plate and watched as Joni ordered two hot dogs, a croissant sandwich, two bags of chips, and a Coke. Gluten allergies, ha! Anyway, Joni was probably going to nibble on one chip and then say how full she was and then Sean would scarf up all the food.

"Don't forget your cheese plate, Miss," said the Amtrak guy, handing it to me and winking.

"Thanks," I said, picking up the plate and squeezing past Joni in the narrow corridor, with a loud *"Pardon."*

Heure 6
I went over the exchange with Joni in my mind and came up with much better things I could have said to her, like, *Thanks for the birthday card—I really appreciated it.* Or, *If everything in the world belonged to me, I wouldn't have told Sean to go out with you.* Or, *Nice cargo pants* (in a sarcastic way).

And so on. It's weird, but for some reason I imagined that when we went on this trip, we'd magically become friends again. I know we were fighting and everything, but I just had this stupid fantasy that it would be like when we were little, when we could fight and say we hated each other, and then the next day be best friends again. So when I got on the train and saw Joni, in her unflattering khaki cargo pants and with her Louis Vuitton luggage, I felt happy, but then when I saw she was totally ignoring me, I realized how stupid my fantasy was.

It's all Sean's fault. None of this would have happened if we hadn't met him. Him and his stupid *love the one you're with* philosophy. I'm never falling in love again, that's for sure.

Heure 7

Sean and Joni came over to our train car to say hi. She obviously hadn't told Sean about the café incident because he was acting like we were all best friends. He took his laptop out and was all excited because he could use it near Ms. G's seat using the train's wireless connection.

"Hey, Ms. G, do you want to see a picture of *poutine*?" He turned the computer toward her.

"Sure," Ms. G said vaguely, glancing up from her book, as if she had forgotten who we were.

Joni stopped glaring at me and smiled at Sean, putting a proprietary hand on his arm.

"What's *poutine*?" she said in the voice of a dumb blonde.

Sean turned his laptop toward Joni so she could see the picture. I couldn't see it from my angle.

"That's gross," squealed Joni, leaning into Sean.

I said, "It's not gross, it's the national dish of Canada: cheese curds on french fries with gravy."

"Well, if it's the national dish, I guess we should experience it," Ms. G said a little hesitantly, looking at the picture. "Although it is a little messy-looking."

I turned to Joni. "With all your allergies, you should probably stay away from it."

Heure 8

Utter boredom. Why did I come on this stupid trip anyway? Joni is impossible. I can't believe that she said that I already had two cheese plates. How dare she? I should have just let her and Sean have their little honeymoon *tout seul*, and stayed home. I still can't believe she never even bothered to respond to any of my e-mails or phone calls. Okay, I know she's dealing with her mom's problems, but doesn't anyone ever worry about my feelings? I'm mad at everyone.

Tried to read *The Decameron*, but it's written very old-fashionedly. It's probably better to read it in the original Italian anyway. Maybe it was because of the train moving, but I started to feel sick to my stomach when the guy described how small tumors under your armpits are called gavoccioli. Gavoccioli sounds like some kind of fancy pasta. *I'll have the gavoccioli al pesto.* Yech. I checked under my arms, but I didn't have any, thank *Dieu*, because if I did, I'd be dead of the Black Plague in forty-eight hours. Thinking about that made me nervous, so instead of reading, I started listening to a podcast by Leticia, my French podcast friend, about going to the cheese store and buying Brebis, which is delicious sheep's milk cheese. I was suddenly starving. Ate remaining stale crackers and cheese crumbs.

Heure 9

Paced the corridors, trying not to fall into people's laps as the train lurched from side to side. Ran into Sean once, by himself. He winked at me, and for a moment I felt that old lifting kind of feeling as he looked at me, his hair flopping over one eye. But then I thought of his lips touching first Joni's and then mine, and I started to feel that he had contaminated both of us. So when he tried to talk to me, I said, "Shhhh," and pointed to the sign about it being the quiet car, which is the car on Amtrak trains where all the really wound-up people like to sit so they can yell at the other people when their cell phones ring.

Heure 10

Too boring to recount, trust me.

Finally, the train ground into the station with much crunching of brakes, and the endless trip was over. I felt grubby and exhausted, like I'd been on the train for days. When we left the train, Ms. G took charge, maneuvering us through the station and herding us into a taxi like sheep. We all squeezed in and sped toward our hostel. I edged my body away from Joni on the sticky vinyl seat so our legs wouldn't touch. I was so tired I didn't even look out the window. Sean and Joni were giggling the whole ride. I had my eyes closed and Ms. G was consulting her map to make sure that the driver didn't take advantage of our Americanism and drive us all around the city.

Première Hostel

After much bumpy driving and weird French hip-hop on the radio, we finally arrived at the hostel, the four of us spilling out of the taxi in a heap. The hostel was in the old city, what they call *Vieux-Montréal*; however, it was not as *charmante* as the photos on the Web site. The hostel was very modern and gray, and there were pages and pages of rules pasted everywhere, like NO SMOKING; NO DRINKING; NO CELL PHONES; NO FOOD IN THE ROOMS; NO PUNGENT FOODS; NO COOKING OF ANY KIND; NO LOUD NOISES AFTER 10; RE- MEMBER, 10–6 IS THE QUIET HOUR; NO ROUGH PLAY OR LEWD BEHAVIOR AT ANY TIME. The signs were in English, French, German, Chinese, and Braille. We filled out a bunch of forms, and then got separated into boys and girls (ha-ha, Joni) and sent to our respective cell blocks (they call them dorms). The beds were thin and hard, and the woman in charge looked at us as if she were deciding what torture method to use to get us to talk. Whenever we asked her something, she said, *"Bon, ben,"* which means "whatever," and in her case meant "there's nothing I can do about it." The three of us were sharing a room, which was weird, but better than being with strangers.

We were exhausted and Ms. G said we should make the best of it, so we lay down on our hard, thin beds. I fell asleep right away, but a few minutes later, I was awakened by a weird sound, like a small cheap fan that had broken down. After a few minutes, I realized it was Joni wheezing. "Are you okay?" I whispered and Joni mumbled no, she thought she was having an allergy attack. "I think these are feather pillows," she whispered ominously. This wheezing thing had happened before, during a Barbie sleepover at my house. A Barbie sleepover, for those of you who had deprived childhoods, is where you eat a lot of junk food and make Barbie do a striptease and have sex with whatever other dolls are lying around, preferably Ken. Once, my mother walked in while Barbie was grinding with Skipper and she said we were very progressive. That night, my parents had to take Joni home because of the wheezing and it was *très* embarrassing for all concerned. Her mom said our house was too dusty, and that was the last time Joni ever slept over. This time, Joni's attack turned out to be a good thing because, after consulting Ms. G's guidebook and using Sean's 3G cell phone to call a gazillion hostels, we finally found a hostel that had room for all of us. We decided we'd wait until the next day to go, since it was already four in the morning.

Our second hostel was in the student quarter, which is called the Latin Quarter. At first, I thought it was a Hispanic area, but then Ms. G explained it was because they used to study Latin. Carpe diem. *Bon, ben.* Whatever. The door to the new hostel was black and covered with graffiti. We rang the bell and a large man came out.

"*Bonjour*, hello, *guten tag*, welcome. *Ça va?* How are you?" He didn't wait for an answer, just led us into a large messy room filled with newspapers, a big golden retriever, and a large cappuccino machine. He had long grayish blond hair in a ponytail, billowy white yoga pants, and bare feet.

"I am Bruno, but you can call me Wolf, yes? You will have wonderful happy time here, yes?"

"What an interesting name," said Ms. G.

"My real name is Bruno, but since I was little boy they

called me Wolf because of these." He bared his teeth and showed us two sharp, pointy teeth on either side of his mouth. "Like werewolf, *nein?*"

We nodded politely. Sean went over to look at his teeth. "Those are awesome."

We introduced ourselves, and Bruno/Wolf put an arm around Sean. "You are lucky man, no, to travel with such beautiful women."

"Yeah, I guess."

"And this is the talented and famous Ornette Coleman," Bruno/Wolf said, pointing at the dog, who was politely holding out his paw to be shaken.

Joni knelt in front of the dog, shaking his paw. "Oh, he's adorable."

Wolf pulled out a pouch of tobacco and methodically started rolling a cigarette, neatly tucking in the loose pieces of tobacco.

Ms. G frowned. "I thought all the hostels were no smoking."

"Don't worry, I don't let the *kinder* smoke, but me, I do what I want. It's my place, *nein?*"

"Do you know that every cigarette you smoke shortens your life by eleven minutes?" lectured Joni.

Wolf took a long drag. "No, but that knowledge is very interesting." He smiled. "These are not mechanical cigarettes, these are organic."

Ms. G said, "Joni, he's a grown man, he can do what he likes."

"I like Gauloises myself," I added.

Wolf laughed, showing his sharp white teeth. He turned

to Ms. G. "This hostel is only one of many business I have. I sell T-shirts: 'Body by *Poutine*.' I sell phone cards. I'm thinking of setting up wireless café with cappuccino. I make you cappuccino later, yes?"

"Yes, that would be lovely," said Ms. G.

"And I show you to your room now, no?"

"No, yes, that would be great," said Joni. "I'm exhausted."

We followed Wolf down a long corridor. I considered whether he might be a good match for Ms. G. He wasn't bad-looking, and he definitely seemed interested in her, and he had a dog, which was always a big plus. We entered a room labeled WOMEN LOUNGING. There were some mattresses on the floor, some posters of Jimi Hendrix and Che Guevara, and an Asian girl painting her nails in the corner in a cloud of incense.

"May I present zee beautiful Sun," said Wolf, bowing at the waist in an exaggerated gesture.

"Hey," said Sean, smiling widely at Sun, who was wearing short shorts, a halter top, and no bra.

"Hey," said Joni, not smiling so much.

"Hello, Sun," said Ms. G, holding out her hand politely. "It's nice to meet you."

"*Bonjour*," I said.

"Nice to meet you guys," said Sun, shaking Ms. G's hand and speaking in a total Valley Girl accent, which kind of disappointed me.

We looked around the room. "I can't sleep on the floor," whispered Joni to Ms. G.

"You are lucky, no?" said Wolf. "We are not so crowded

now, although we are best hostel"— he pronounced it *hostile*—"in world. You don't have to share beds. We have bathrooms, showers, sinks, Wi-Fi, Nescafé, everything you need. Yes?" He motioned to Sean. "I show you the men's lounging." He shrugged. "Separate for the guys and dolls—rules, you know?"

Sean and Wolf disappeared, and Joni, Ms. G, and I carefully put our stuff in the old green gym lockers that were provided for storage.

"Do you think it's safe here?" Ms. G asked, putting her purse inside a locker that had no lock.

Joni looked skeptical.

"Sure," I said, wanting to reassure her.

"It's totally safe," said Sun. "Everyone is very chill around here."

"Where are you from?" asked Joni, waving away the incense smoke with an unnecessarily large motion.

"Sorry about the smoke. Venice Beach, California. You guys?"

"Brooklyn, New York."

"Brooklyn—that's very cool. I used to know a guy named Brooklyn."

I yawned. "Sorry to be rude, but I'm exhausted. We hardly slept last night."

"No problem, I'm going out anyway."

As soon as Sun left, Joni blew out the incense.

I lay down on the mattress in all my clothes, and woke up four hours later.

I barely had a chance to wash up before Ms. G called a meeting in the Main Lounging, which was a room with some beat-up sofas, an old desktop computer, and a mini fridge. Wolf brought in a tray with coffee and cheese sandwiches, which we all devoured. There was a gavel lying around and Sean picked it up. "I call this meeting to order." He banged the gavel loudly on the table.

Ms. G said, "Thanks, Sean. So, I know you guys probably thought once we got here, we'd all wander off and do our own thing, but I am responsible for you, and since we did receive school funding, we need to do culturally relevant activities and report on them. So I thought we would each plan out an itinerary for every day we're here. I'll take the first day, Joni the next day, then Sean, then Lotus. I've done some research and written up an itinerary for tomorrow, and Wolf has a copy machine, so we can make copies later." She handed each of us a guidebook to Montreal.

We read the guidebooks and local papers for a while. In one of the papers, I glanced at an ad for a reading at Chapters Bookstore. I couldn't believe it. It was a reading by Mireille, the author of *FWDGF*, right here in Montreal! How could I not have known about this? It's on Sean's day, at 7:30 p.m. I'll just have to cut out early from whatever we're doing. I am *not* going to miss it. I wonder if Mireille will know who I am from my letters.

Later, Ms. G took us all out for dinner, to a nearby restaurant that Wolf had recommended. It was a noisy pub-like kind of restaurant with five thousand beers on the menu and ten types of mussels. I got a cheese plate, Ms. G and Sean got mussels, and Joni got a *salade*. I told Ms. G to try a beer. "Since you're the only one who can drink legally."

"Okay, you pick for me, Lotus."

I picked one called *Trip de Schoune* because it had a cool name. It looked golden and delicious, but Ms. G wouldn't let us have any. Sean examined the bottle. "You know, this is pretty high alcohol content, compared with American beers."

"Uh-oh," said Ms. G. "But it doesn't taste strong."

"It's good," said Joni, sneaking a sip of beer when Ms. G went to the ladies' room.

"So, Sean, what do you have in store for us on your day?" asked Ms. G when she got back.

"Well, I thought I'd take us through some of Montreal's history and unique cuisine, but it's a surprise."

The waitress brought Ms. G another beer, and I had another Diet Pepsi and an order of french fries. Sean had more mussels because it was all-you-can-eat.

Joni turned to me. "Why do you bother with the diet soda when you're eating french fries?"

I took a french fry and chewed it slowly. "I just like the taste better," I told her, which was true, although she looked at me like she thought I was lying.

When we got back to the hostel, Wolf and Sun were playing a kids' version of Trivial Pursuit. Sun was winning.

"Hey, you guys want to play?" she asked.

"Sure," said Sean, and then Joni gave him a look and he said, "Maybe some other time."

"We're going to go work on our itineraries," murmured Joni as they disappeared.

Wolf pulled up a chair for Ms. G and motioned us to sit down. We started playing, and Ms. G and Sun got almost all the questions right. I got a couple right, and Wolf got most of them wrong. It didn't seem to bother him. He started to pour us all some clear liquid, which he said was a pear liqueur. When Ms. G protested, he said he was only giving us a drop. "It's nothing, *c'est rien, nada, niente, nein*, yes?"

Ms. G put her hand up to stop him. "They're underage and I'm responsible for them, so while they're here . . ."

Wolf shrugged and put away the bottle.

Sun told me that she was waiting for some friends who were coming to Montreal in a couple of days. She said she had been traveling around Canada for months and she loved it, and that she could never settle down. She told me she was thinking of writing a guide to the world for bikers on a low budget. When she said the word *bikers* I sort of tuned out and stopped listening, but then she said something about Sean, and I woke up.

"Sean's pretty hot," she said, playing with her long straight hair, twisting it up into a messy bun and then untwisting it.

"Yeah, he is pretty cute," I agreed.

"He's going out with your friend, right? The *skinny* girl." (Why is it that skinny girls always call each other *skinny* in this disapproving way, even though they are just as skinny?)

"Yeah, they are going out," I said. "Kind of. But it's not serious or anything." I couldn't help myself.

We stopped playing the game after a while. Ms. G said it was late and we should go to bed. Wolf tried to get us to stay and play poker, but we were all too tired. Joni wasn't there when we got back to the Women Lounging. Ms. G asked if I'd go look for her. I hesitated and Sun offered to go. A few minutes later, Sun appeared with Joni in tow.

"I found her," said Sun, her arm around Joni as if she and Joni were old friends. "She was with Sean." She winked at Joni. "You two are so adorable together. Like puppies."

"Stop it," said Joni, pulling away from Sun. "Please."

"Oh, the puppy has a temper!"

"Can you please stop calling me a puppy."

Sun gave a little bark. "Okay."

eleven

Montreal, *Jour* 1

Ms. G's day started way too early, with us trudging to take the subway to an unknown location. Finally, we arrived at some kind of bakery.

"Here we are," said Ms. G, as if we were at the Taj Mahal.

"I can't believe I've come all the way to Montreal to eat a squished-looking bagel," I protested a few minutes later, poking my finger into my oddly shaped item. We were in a bagel shop in a neighborhood called Outremont, supposedly having the quintessential Montreal experience. For some reason, I didn't expect to see Jewish people outside of New York, as if we had a monopoly on them, but there were the same Amish-looking Hasidic girls with incredibly long skirts who looked like they had never seen the sun. My so-called bagel was weird, like a bagel that had been tortured on the rack or forced to mate with a bialy. It didn't taste bad, but it wasn't what I considered a bagel. It was just a squashed, slightly sweet bready thing, with a large hole in the middle.

"I kind of like them," said Joni, taking a small bite and sliding closer to Sean.

"Apparently there was a large Jewish influence in Montreal. Quebec was also a large center for fur trading," said Ms. G in her teacher voice.

"I think wearing fur is wrong," said Joni, still nibbling on a corner of her plain bagel.

"But you eat meat, so what's the difference?" I said, spreading some butter on mine. "And you wear leather shoes."

Joni ignored me and started reading from the paper the bagels were wrapped in. "The bagel was introduced to Montreal by a baker named Engelman who arrived in the city from Russia in 1919; his descendants continue to make bagels today."

"They're not so bad," said Sean, going up to the counter to get another one.

"Outremont is such a cool name," I said to no one in particular.

When Sean got back, I said, "You're so Outremont."

"What?"

"I just made it up—it means weird or whatever you want it to."

Sean and Joni adopted my new word immediately and loudly. They are such followers.

"Your bagel is totally Outremont," Joni said to Sean, as he slathered on cream cheese and lox and tomato.

Sean countered with, "Your face is totally Outremont."

"What about when something's good?" asked Ms. G.

I thought about this for a moment. "Oh, that would be Plateau. That's the neighborhood with all the good bars and restaurants I was reading about in the guidebook. Like, this coffee is totally Plateau."

Joni and Sean continued to be ridiculously Outremont, while Ms. G and I discussed books and movies. I eavesdropped at a table of *Montréaliens* who were sitting next to us. They were speaking mostly in French, with a few words in English, but I could barely understand anything they were saying. They spoke nothing like Leticia.

After breakfast, Ms. G's itinerary was nonstop. We went to the Museum of Contemporary Art and saw some cool abstract paintings by Quebec artists and some weird neon paintings by an American guy named Bruce something, which were not that interesting to *moi*, although some of them had neon pictures of guys with penises and Joni and Sean couldn't stop giggling about them. They are so immature. Then we went to the history museum and saw some exhibits of furs and old Indian artifacts. Afterward, we trekked to a famous tea store, where I had some delicious blueberry tea and Ms. G had something odd called rooibos and Sean and Joni had hot chocolate. I kept trying to speak French, but everyone kept speaking English back to me, I guess to be polite or because they're embarrassed by their weird French Canadian accents. After the tea, we were hungry, so we stopped at a pastry store and I had something chocolaty, which I can't remember the name of, and Ms. G had a *chausson aux pommes*, which is like an apple turnover, and Sean and Joni split a coffee éclair and ended up with cream all over their faces. I don't know why, but everything tastes better here.

After the pastries, we walked down to the old city where they have cool cobblestoned streets, but too many tourists and the same annoying Peruvian street musicians you see everywhere. We looked at some boring historic buildings and got hazelnut gelato. Then we went into a bunch of touristy shops where they were selling little Inuit animal sculptures and weird furs. Inuits are apparently the native people of Canada. I bought a couple of little sculptures for my parents, one for Adam, and one for Barbara from the Wellness Center. Then we were all exhausted, so we decided to go back to the hostel and rest.

When we finally got back, Wolf was outside the hostel smoking and sitting on a beach chair with a small umbrella set up next to him. He had just rolled a cigarette, but when he lit it, there was a sweet smell, which made me suspect there was something besides tobacco in that handwoven pouch. When he saw us, he put it out. I recognized the music playing on his boom box as "Aqualung," by Jethro Tull, because it's one of my dad's favorite songs. Wolf looked incredibly happy to see us.

"My Americans," he said, giving Sean a high five and

patting me and Joni on the shoulder. He kissed Ms. G once on each cheek, which made her blush.

I went to lie down on my mattress. Sean and Joni went off somewhere, to fool around, no doubt, and Ms. G stayed in the lounge with Wolf, who wanted to try out his new cappuccino machine on her. Sun was out, so there was only a faint smell of incense in the air.

I worked on my *pensées sur Montréal* (thoughts about Montreal):

> All the old men (40 and over) here wear their hair in ponytails. If they were on What Not to Wear, Nick the hairdresser would immediately cut them off and they would look twenty years younger. A gray ponytail is a terrible accessory.
>
> The French accent is very hard to understand here. I think it must be some peculiar dialect.
>
> They are obsessed with maple syrup here. Not sure why.
>
> There are bicycles everywhere and the guys wear those creepy tight bicycle shorts, just like in Brooklyn.
>
> Great pastries, coffee, chocolate. I could really stick to my FWDGF diet here, except for the frites.
>
> There's a giant cross that looms over the city, kind of creepy, like in a vampire movie.
>
> Guys in Montreal are cute, very metrosexual, to the point where it's hard to tell if some of them are straight or gay.

After a while, I got bored with *pensée*-ing and started reading a guidebook to figure out the itinerary for my day. I read a short history of Montreal. I was shocked by what I read. Originally, there were Indians living here, like in the United States, and then a guy named Cartier (like the store) came over from France to make money off the furs—and all the maple syrup, I guess—and then the British people came and told everyone they couldn't be French anymore and took all their money. So now the British people still have most of the money, and the French people are still mad and that's why they make all the road signs and parking meters in French. No wonder the people haven't been that friendly to *moi*. They probably think I'm one of those evil British people who stole their maple syrup. I also learned that the motto they have on the license plates, *Je Me Souviens* (I Remember), is from a poem that says, "I'm French, no matter what you British people do to me."

The four of us went to *typique* bistro for dinner. I decided to order in French. I told the waitress, *"Je prends la crêpe au fromage de chèvre et champignons sauvages, s'il vous plaît, et je suis desolée que ces Anglais vous ont volé votre argent."* (I'll have the wild mushroom crêpes with goat cheese and I'm very sorry that those British people stole all your money.)

The waitress replied in perfect English, "Thank you, I will get your crêpes right away," which was sort of disappointing, but I felt we had reached an understanding. Joni ordered roast salmon on a bed of lentils. Ms. G got roast chicken with *frites* and a beer called the End of the World (*la Fin du Monde*). Sean got *lapin*, which I told Joni meant rabbit, and we both said at once how disgusting it was and then remembered we weren't friends anymore.

"Think of it as chicken," said Ms. G, musing, "although when you start thinking about eating chicken too much, it all starts to seem a little odd. Maybe it's best just not to think about these things."

"Like when they ask you if you want a breast or a thigh," I said. "How weird is that?"

"Or skin," said Joni.

"It's very Outremont," said Sean.

After dinner, Sean wanted to go hear *le jazz*, but we were all too tired. You think you are going to do all these things when you travel, but then all the travel and newness makes you tired and it's all you can do to eat pastries, drink coffee, and go lie down. When we went back to the Women Lounging, Sun was there, reading a book by Pema Chödrön, a Zen Buddhist. She showed it to me and Ms. G, although Joni pretended to not be interested.

"It's all about showing loving kindness to yourself," said Sun.

"Can you guys be quiet, I'm trying to sleep," said Joni, who had a pillow over her head.

Wrote postcard to parents:

Chers parents,

I am writing as promised. Quelle surprise, right? Yes, I got here okay; yes, the place we're staying is fine, although the beds are on the floor; no, I do not have enough money, Canada is très expensive, so if you want to advance me my allowance or inheritance, please feel free!

I would have called when I got here, but you still haven't allowed me to have a cell phone, which makes me kind of an anomaly (I know—SAT word) among kids my age.

We are doing masses of cultural activity and I am absorbing lots of French, although not speaking so much (will explain later). Would bring you back delicious pastries, but they probably would be stale by the time they got there.

Joni and Sean are fine (disgusting and couply, but fine) and Ms. G is very responsible—am hoping to fix her up with German owner of hostel (will keep you informed)—am hoping he doesn't have Nazi relatives like in Suite Française.

Grosses bises (that means big kisses, not gross kisses),

I remain,

Your daughter,

Lotus

twelve

Montreal, *Jour* 2

When I woke up in the morning, I was alone in Women Lounging. Or so I thought. As I stretched and yawned and navigated myself up from my uncomfortable futon on the floor, I saw Sun doing yoga on the other side of the room, totally naked. She was leaning over in what I recognized as Triangle Pose and I couldn't help looking at her "hooha" as my *grand-mère* calls it, the hair of which had been trimmed into the shape of a yin/yang symbol.

Sun saw me looking, but didn't seem the slightest bit

embarrassed. She moved into Warrior Pose, her legs and arms outstretched. "Oh, do you like it? I found a great waxer in downtown Montreal; I could give you her name if you're interested."

"No, that's okay."

"Guys prefer it." Sun was now moving into Downward Dog.

I felt annoyed. "Guys prefer a lot of things. So what?"

"You should be the one doing yoga," said Sun, kicking her legs up easily into a headstand.

"Why, because of my name?" I said sarcastically, staring at the poster of Che Guevara so I wouldn't accidentally look at her again.

"Yeah. Wow, this feels great, I could stay up here forever. It really changes your perspective."

"Well, knock yourself out. I'm going to go get breakfast." I made sure to close the door behind me so no one would be subjected to her nudity, especially Sean.

Wolf had made breakfast and everyone was sitting around the tiny kitchen table. He put out pumpernickel bread, two different kinds of cheese, liverwurst in a tube, and a big slab of butter. Joni was buttering a piece of bread for Sean (she never eats butter) and Ms. G was chatting happily about the inadequacy of the U.S. health-care system with Wolf. He seemed surprisingly well informed for some-one who lived in another country. It was like being home with my parents discussing politics at the breakfast table. Wolf came over to me. "Coffee?" he asked, espresso pot in hand.

"Yes, *s'il vous plaît*."

Wolf put a cup of steaming black coffee and a small container of condensed milk in front of me as I sat down.

I examined the milk can. "What is this? Don't you have real milk here?"

"My parents got used to it during the war, so we always had it. Now I prefer it."

I asked, "Hey, Wolf, were you in Germany when they had rationing?"

Wolf turned to Ms. G and made a sad clown face. "Do I look that old?"

"No, not at all. Anyway, Lotus, I think they drank ersatz coffee during the war, with chicory," said Ms. G.

"I love that word, *ersatz*," said Joni.

"Good SAT word, as my *mère* would say," I added.

No one was eating the liverwurst, but Wolf insisted that I try it anyway. I mushed it around my plate and hid it under some pumpernickel. Sean asked where Sun was and I said I thought she had gone out for a walk.

"I was thinking we should invite her today, just to be friendly," he said, looking all innocent.

I shook my head. "I think I've seen quite enough of Sun today," I said, trying to avoid the picture in my head. "Anyway, she told me she was going for a really, really long walk, so . . ."

After breakfast, Joni directed us to the metro and we got out and walked for what seemed like hours to get to the gigantic Mount Royal Park (that's the park with the giant, creepy, glittered-out cross on top of it). Joni said it was designed by the same guy who designed Prospect Park. *Quel* small world.

According to the guidebook, what you're supposed to do is take the metro to the top and walk back down, but what we did (*merci*, Joni) was take the metro to the bottom and hike up Boulevard Saint-Laurent to the beginning of the park. It would have been nice, except it was a gazillion degrees, they were doing massive construction, I was sweating, and my wedge *sandales* were not *merci*-ing me. I think Joni wanted to hike up the big hill because she was afraid she'd been eating too many pastries and had gained an ounce, especially now that we're around Sun, who looks like a supermodel.

We finally got to the park, walked for a mile inside, and found this little pond called Beaver Lake. There were ducks wandering around everywhere like they owned the place, not to mention stressed-out mothers with sloppy children, and couples in love.

Me and Ms. G stayed in the shady part with the other non-couple, non-baby people and the squirrels, some of which were *très* aggressive and tried to climb on the table. At least they didn't have the rule that you can't eat anything like in the Botanic Garden, because I had some *poutine*-flavored potato chips I wanted to try. The park made me think about that afternoon when Sean and I lay in the grass—our relationship was so perfect for around twelve seconds. I looked over at him and Joni walking around Beaver Lake (that sounds dirty, doesn't it?) and made a decision never to like anyone that much again.

"Hey, Ms. G, whatever happened with you and Man One? He seemed to really like you."

"We went out a couple of times, but . . ." She shrugged. "It was nice, but . . ."

"What, no spark? No love connection? Was he a bad kisser?"

Ms. G smiled. "No, he was fine. We just didn't click, I guess. It's okay, Lotus, don't look so disappointed."

"Well, there's a lot of *poisson* in the sea, as my *grand-mère* says."

"No," Ms. G said, shooing away a squirrel, "what I'm trying to say is that I'm actually quite content on my own. I belong to a chorus and a book group. I go on trips. I have friends and my books. Not everyone is destined to be part of a couple."

I patted her on the arm. "Don't worry—we'll find you someone. How about Wolf? Except for that bizarre ponytail, he's kind of cute."

Ms. G shook her head. "Lotus, don't be ridiculous."

"Why, what's wrong with him?"

"He's . . . I don't know. He's not my type."

"He's male. He has a thing for you. He's not bad-looking, so why not? Hey, did you bring your makeup with you? I noticed you weren't wearing it after I went to all that trouble."

"I know, I'm sorry. I just don't have the time, I guess. And he does not have a thing for me."

"Hey, I have a *chouette* idea: On my day, we're going to go shopping."

"And how is that culturally relevant?"

"What could be more culturally relevant than knowing what the real *Montréaliennes* are wearing this season?

Anyway, fashion is culture. Didn't you see *The Devil Wears Prada*? Or *Ugly Betty,* or *Zoolander,* or *America's Next Top Model*? Although it seems shallow, fashion is very deep."

"Hmmm. Interesting theory, Lotus."

"Oh, and I wanted to let you know that tomorrow, on Sean's day, I'm going to have to leave early to go to a book reading."

"That sounds interesting. Maybe we could all go."

"Trust me, no one else will want to go. It's for *French Women Don't Get Fat*."

"Oh. Well, I suppose that would be all right if you went by yourself, provided it's nearby and you take a taxi back."

We sat there quietly, brushing away the little gnats that kept flying over, and looking at Sean and Joni, who were now holding hands, which was only a little painful to watch.

Ms. G took a couple of potato chips from the bag. "I noticed you and Joni are still . . . estranged. I'm sorry. I guess I thought this trip would help."

"I know, me too. It's like before, we were in this magic circle together. And inside the magic circle, we were best friends, and outside was everyone else. It was us against the world. And now we've stepped out of the magic circle." I put on my best German model accent. "As Heidi Klum says, 'You're either in or you're out.' "

"Is your rift because of Sean?"

"I guess it was initially. But now it's like we're both mad, and I don't even know what we're mad about."

"Maybe you're mad that you're no longer friends."

"Maybe."

I started to read the Montreal guidebook, but there were

so many places to see that I felt overwhelmed and had to stop reading. Ms. G and I decided to walk around the lake too. We caught up with Joni and Sean, who wanted to feed the ducks his leftover croissant. There was a sign that said it was *interdit,* which I explained meant forbidden, but he said that was totally Outremont. He fed them anyway. Then, dozens of ducks crowded around us and Ms. G said it was like the movie *The Birds* and Joni started to worry about bird flu.

"Just don't kiss them," I said helpfully.

Joni and Sean ran off again. I felt like Ms. G and I were the parents of two rambunctious toddlers. When they came back, there were both talking about how great the lake was, how much they loved Montreal, how they had played Frisbee with some kids from McGill University, how there was an ice cream truck and they wanted to get some.

I had a sudden urge to get away from them. "Hey, do you guys smell something burning? I'm going to go check it out." I came back after a few minutes of pacing around and announced, "Why is it that no matter how far you travel, you always see people barbecuing? I'll bet that if we ever got those stupid spaceships to the moon and spent some quality time there, someone would immediately start barbecuing. Is barbecuing some basic human instinct like shopping and having children?"

"The moon isn't actually a planet," corrected Joni.

"Tell it to the College Board. I don't care."

"Would you two stop being so Outremont," said Sean.

"You know, there's another area called Westmount too," said Ms. G.

"I thought that was the same thing as Outremont," said Sean.

"No, *outre* means *out there*, not *West*," I corrected him. "Westmount is where all the British robber barons live and refuse to learn French," I added.

"I think that's a bit of a simplification," said Ms. G.

"Okay, so when something's totally messed up, even more than Outremont, we'll call it Westmount," decided Sean.

"Okay," agreed Joni.

"Let's get out of this park, it's totally Westmount," I said.

"*D'accord*," agreed Sean, "as soon as I get an ice cream." He ran over to the truck.

"Me too," said Joni, running after him.

Chère Grand-mère,

Survived second day in Montreal. Went to the park, walked many miles, was almost attacked by possibly rabid squirrels. Went to the Botanical Garden, walked around more in hot sun, hopefully had enough organic sunscreen on. Had to watch Joni and Sean canoodling, as you would say.

For dinner we went to a pizza place called Pizzadelic. It was the kind of pizza place where you can get pineapple and cheeseburger on a pizza, but I had a quatre fromages (four-cheese) pizza, which was pas mal at all. Sun went along—she's this girl who's being all friendly to Joni, telling her she likes her cargo pants, but she really likes Sean, if you know what I mean. She started telling us about her boyfriend, who is some kind of crazy marathoner, but I think she was just trying to make Sean jealous.

The best part of today was the Butterfly Pavilion, where you go into this futuristic white tent and are surrounded by butterflies that fly around you and you can feel it when they brush by you with their silky wings. I could have stayed in there forever.

That reminds me: Didn't we see an old movie called Butterflies Are Free on the AMC channel? With Kate Hudson's mother, where she was a hippie and with that blind guy? Anyway, I was thinking of you today.

Your faithful granddaughter,

Lotus

thirteen

Montreal, *Jour* 3 (and the day of the *FWDGF* reading!)

Sean has been feverishly researching *poutine* on Montreal Web sites and his plan for the day involves searching for the best *poutine* in all of Montreal.

"You could be like the Rachael Ray of *poutine*," I said.

"I see myself more as the Anthony Bourdain of *poutine*," said Sean, trying to look taller.

"He is kind of charming, isn't he," said Ms. G.

To prepare us for our adventure, Sean read us some factoids about *poutine*, or *poutin*oids as I called them.

"Okay, so, the earliest date associated with its invention

is 1957, which is when this guy Fernand Lachance said that a customer at his restaurant, L'Idéal, requested french fries and cheese together in a bag, to which the restaurateur responded: '*Ça va faire une maudite poutine*' ('That's going to make a damn mess'). Adding sauce to the cheese curds and fries was a later innovation. The owner of another restaurant, a guy named Jean-Paul Roy, also claims the title of 'the Inventor of Poutine,' dating his claim from 1964. Roy's claim stems from his having made a potato sauce, which he was slathering on fries sold in his restaurant. He also sold bags of cheddar cheese curds, which were a common snack in the region. He noticed customers were adding the cheese curds to his fries and sauce. Soon after, he made the combination a regular menu item."

"Nice research," said Ms. G.

"Wikipedia," said Sean, "and I found this cool Web site, the Midnight *Poutine*, that rates all the different places on the quality of their *poutine*."

"Thrilling," I said, yawning loudly.

I don't know if you've ever had *poutine*, but after trekking to several greasy spoons and having a bunch of different varieties (for example, *poutine italienne* with marinara sauce, *poutine Sainte-Perpétue* with fried onions and bacon, and, of course, classic *poutine* with slimy curds and brown gravy, which looks sort of predigested), we were all feeling bloated and sick and couldn't care less which one was the best. I pretended to eat most of mine, smushing the french fries into the weird sauces. Ms. G seemed to be doing the same thing, but Joni was actually eating hers, trying to show Sean what a good sport she was.

The only other cultural activity Sean had planned was searching for the birthplaces and haunts of famous *Montréaliennes*, including Leonard Cohen, William Shatner, and the Kids in the Hall, who are apparently some comedy group. After trudging around boring Shatner Hall at McGill University, we voted not to search for the other famous Montrealers.

"I don't think the Kids in the Hall are actually from Montreal anyway," conceded Sean.

"Sean, I can't believe you're a Trekkie," I said, teasing him.

"I'm not. My dad and I used to watch the reruns when I was little, that's all."

"That's cute," said Joni.

"Live long and prosper," I said, twisting my fingers into the Vulcan greeting.

"I always liked Sulu," said Ms. G.

"I liked Jean-Luc Picard," said Joni.

"I prefer Dr. Who," I offered, "or that cute guy from *Firefly*."

"So, what else do you have planned for us, Sean?" asked Ms. G.

Sean had many ideas, none of which we ended up doing, including:

Casino: vetoed because of age issue.

Beer tasting: again, vetoed because of age issue.

White-water rafting on the Lachine Rapids—voted against for a number of reasons: too dangerous, too expensive, might get wet, too much trouble.

We finally decided to go to a movie. I had been saving

this for my Montreal day, but things were devolving rapidly, and I was exhausted from all the walking around, so I gave it to Sean. Luckily, there was a French film festival going on that I happened to have the schedule for. I decided that after the movie, I would still have plenty of time to get to the reading. For the people whose French was not so good (everyone but *moi*), I found a film in French with English *sous-titres*. It was a Swiss film about a family who lived in a very large, depressing apartment building and how each person saw the events of a single *journée*. During the scene where the husband was having sex with the neighbor, I heard whispering from where Joni and Sean were sitting.

"Shhh," I said.

I saw Joni get up from her seat and, at first, I thought she and Sean were having a fight. Instinctively, I got up and followed her out to the hallway. When I didn't see her anywhere, I went to look for her in the bathroom.

"Hey, Joni, are you in here?"

I heard the unmistakable sounds of someone getting sick. After a couple of minutes, the sounds subsided and I knocked on the stall door.

"Joni, are you okay?"

"Do I sound okay?"

"Can I get you anything?"

"No, I just want to go home."

She came out of the stall looking pale and tiny, and washed her face a million times. I gave her a stick of gum.

"I'll go in and tell them we're leaving, okay? We can take a cab back."

"You don't need to come with me," said Joni, not looking at me.

"You want me to get Sean or Ms. G?"

Joni shook her head stubbornly. "No, I'm fine by myself."

"Let me just tell Ms. G, okay?"

Joni nodded. I ran back to the theater and whispered to Sean what had happened. He wanted to leave, but I told him Joni just wanted me to come with her. I told Ms. G and she whispered, "What about your reading? Do you want me to go with Joni?"

I wanted to go to the reading really, really badly, but this was my chance to do something for Joni. I figured I'd take her home, and then, if I was really quick, I could still make it to the reading.

"I'll figure something out," I whispered.

I took a cab with Joni, against her wishes, back to the hostel. She didn't look so hot, so I figured it was better if I stayed at the hostel, even if she still did hate me. She went inside and I went to the nearest drugstore and got her the Canadian version of Pepto-Bismol. Sun was in the kitchen when I got back. She offered to make some tea and bring it in to Joni.

I went to check on Joni after a little while. Sun had gone all Clara Barton visiting nurse on her, putting cool towels on her forehead.

"Hey, you want some pot, Joni?" asked Sun. "I hear that's good for nausea."

"No, she doesn't want pot," I answered, annoyed. "Joni, I brought you some ginger ale."

"Thanks." Joni seemed friendlier now. Probably she was just too weak to be mad.

"How are you feeling?"

Joni looked a little bit more alive than at the movie theater. "A little better."

"You're going to have to go to *Poutine* Anonymous."

"Don't make me laugh, my stomach still hurts."

I sat there till Joni went to sleep. When I looked at the clock, it was already nine.. The reading had started at 7:30, so it was way too late to try to go. I was disappointed, but I felt good about staying with Joni, in a kind of Mother Teresa way.

fourteen

Lotus *jour*

"Today is the *jour de* Lotus and today, *aujourd'hui,* we are not having liverwurst," I told Wolf.

He looked confused. "But I thought you loved the liverwurst."

"No, I love the cheese and the bread and the coffee and the butter, but I do *not* love the liverwurst."

Wolf removed the offending tube. "Okay, you can do what you like, Wolf does not care, it's a free country, *nein?*"

"Yes, it is. At least I think it is. Okay, everybody," I said, "today, *après* breakfast, we are going shopping downtown."

Sean groaned. Joni looked sort of interested, Ms. G, kind of skeptical.

Shopping was a little stressful, because the Canadian dollar was much more robust than anticipated. I thought everything would be a bargain, but apparently socialism is more economically sound than capitalism.

"I'm surprised you didn't know about the exchange rate," said Joni, "being a journalist and all."

"I'm not a financial journalist," I told her. "I'm more of a lifestyle reporter."

"Like on *Entertainment Tonight*."

"No, like on some much more prestigious news show, like on CNN, or for a blog like Gothamist."

Joni was the only one who was unfazed by the prices, and she bought a pair of overpriced long shorts and a weird pouffy-sleeved shirt. I thought there would be more interesting fashions here, but they had the same midget *Little House on the Prairie* styles that were currently in vogue in New York: tiny shrunken wraps, dolman sleeves, and balloon skirts that look like bad laundry accidents.

Since it was raining, we descended into the underground city, which is a giant subterranean mall, although Joni was worried about an earthquake and even I was feeling claustrophobic as we descended farther and farther underground. We ended up at a store called Club Monaco, which they have in New York, but was much bigger here. I felt like I was Tim Gunn, crossing my arms and putting on a pained expression while Ms. G picked out clothes that were way too old-fashioned and baggy.

"These will not do," I said sternly. "They are exactly like the baggy clothes that you had on when we got here." I sent Ms. G back into the dressing room with a pile of new outfits, including a navy wraparound dress, which she thought was much too tight, and a black pencil skirt. Even Joni thought she looked really good, although Sean had disappeared, so we didn't get the male opinion. Then we went to the makeup counter and I bought her some mineral powder and red organic lip stain, which she didn't want to accept, but I told her I was using my cupcake money and didn't want to hear about it.

"You need to look good for tonight, right?"

"What are you talking about?" asked Joni, fingering one of those short twisty sweaters that looks like it was made for someone with shrunken arms.

"I'm making dinner for Ms. G and Wolf tonight. Oh yeah, when you were passed out last night *après* the *poutine* incident, we all played poker and Ms. G was out of chips, so Wolf bet her dinner. And I said I would prepare a *French Women Don't Get Fat* feast."

Ms. G looked nervous. "I didn't think you were serious, Lotus."

"Oh, I'm serious. I'm very serious." I brushed some blush on the apples of her cheeks, trying to find the perfect color.

Joni rolled her eyes. "I can't believe I missed everything! Sun gave me a pill to help me sleep."

"I'll bet she did," I said, picking up some mascara and an eyelash curler.

After shopping, we met up with Sean for lunch at a Greek restaurant. Sean told Joni what happened in the movie that we missed and I had flaming Kasseri cheese and all the waiters said, "Opa!"

After lunch, we went to the Jean-Talon Market so I could pick up supplies for dinner. Ms. G kept trying to pay for stuff, but I stopped her. The market was incredible: It had spices, cheese and more cheese, maple syrup, and the most amazing fruit and vegetables, all beautifully arranged in tiny wicker baskets. I got everything I needed for the dinner and it didn't even cost that much. While me and Ms. G shopped, Joni and Sean ran up and down the aisles like two-year-olds. After I was done, we all ate apple crêpes with whipped cream at this little stand, and the crêpe guy told me I was *jolie* (pretty).

Back at the hostel, while everyone else was resting, I transformed the dingy computer/living room into a beautiful dining room. I vacuumed and neatened, and put my favorite toile scarf on the table for a tablecloth. I also put a red scarf around the lamp like they do in old movies and hoped it wouldn't start a fire. But when I began taking out my dinner ingredients, I realized I was missing an essential part of my recipe. *"Merde."*

At that moment, Sun came down the stairs, fully clothed for once.

"Hey, Sun, you don't happen to have any champagne, do you?"

"No, but I could get you some."

"That would be amazing." I gave Sun some money and

asked her to get champagne, wine, and an after-dinner drink.

She disappeared for a little while into the back and came out with Sean. "See you soon."

That wasn't exactly what I had in mind, but I really needed the champagne. A while later, Joni came down. She wandered around the table, picking up a fork and straightening it.

"Hey, do you want to help? I mean, not me, but for Ms. G?"

Joni shrugged. "Okay."

"Can you handle the *salade*? I have the recipe here and all the ingredients. It would be a really big help."

"Sure. Hey, have you seen Sean?"

"Yeah, he and Sun went to go get the wine and champagne."

Joni made a face. "Why didn't you ask me to go?"

"I know, I know, but Sun had a fake ID and you were sleeping."

While Joni made the *salade*, I went into the Women Lounging. Ms. G was putting on the navy wrap dress I had gotten her. It fit her perfectly and made her waist look tiny.

I looked her over, made her turn around. "Good, just some more mascara and lip gloss."

"Are you sure? I don't want to look too . . . you know."

"Too what?"

"You know, trying too hard . . . too available."

"Too hoochie mama, you mean. No, don't worry, you're perfect. But you do need something." I adjusted the dress and added a necklace. "I'm beginning to understand what Rachel Zoe goes through."

"Who?"

"Just some annoying troll-like stylist to the stars. She has a reality show on Bravo."

"I guess I need to watch more TV to keep up," said Ms. G.

"No, stick with AMC and the History Channel. It would be too much of a shock to your system to watch real television."

I sprayed a cloud of an organic lavender fragrance I got at the Wellness Center and had Ms G. walk through it. "Do you know that Coco Chanel said a woman who doesn't wear perfume has no future?"

"No, I didn't, Lotus."

"Okay—stay here and don't rub off your makeup. We'll come get you when we're ready."

Ms. G nodded. "I can't believe I'm doing this."

"And remember, just forget that we're going back to New York soon and that you probably won't ever see him again and that he's not your type, and try to have a good time, okay?"

"I'll try. And Lotus, I just wanted to say that was really nice what you did for Joni yesterday. Does she know you missed your book reading?"

"No, and don't tell her."

"Why?"

"I don't know." I thought about it for a second. "I guess I don't want Joni to feel like she has to be nice to me because I missed the reading."

I ran back to the kitchen. Joni had arranged the pear slices into a fan on each plate and was placing the hazelnuts around the center.

"Wow, that looks great, Joni!"

"Do you think that's enough nuts?"

"*Oui*, it's *parfait*."

Sean came in with the liquor. Joni went and stood near Sean and he put his arm around her. Unfortunately, Sun came in right after Sean, with a cheery "Hey, can I help, girls?"

"Maybe you can put these candles on the table." I gave her some honey candles I got at the Jean-Talon Market. "And dim the lights, okay? Try to make it *romantique*."

Sun lit the candles, while Joni arranged some wildflowers she found outside in little jars like we'd seen on Nigella Lawson's show. I opened the wine and put out the canapés, some little pastry things I got at the bakery. (Okay, so it wasn't a *totally* home-cooked meal.) We were all working like *chiens* and Sean was just sitting there reading the *Montreal Mirror*. Typical male. I'll bet J.P. stood around while Simone de Beauvoir set the table too.

He put down the paper. "You know what we should do tonight? See if we can get tickets to see Rufus Wainright."

"That sounds great," purred Sun.

"He's from Montreal, so it's extra cultural," said Sean. "We should all go, right?"

"I can't," I said. "I'm in charge of this dinner. Nothing will happen unless I stay."

Joni looked at me, and then into the dining room, and then at Sean. I could see she was struggling to decide whether to stay. Sean did nothing to convince her either way.

"You should go," I said. "I'm fine here."

"But I want to see what happens. With Wolf and Ms. G. You guys go, I'm fine here."

"Are you sure?" said Sean.

"Yeah," said Joni, uncertainly.

When they were gone, I turned to Joni, who was neatening up the kitchen.

"Are you sure about this? Letting Sun go out with Sean?"

"Why do you care?"

"I don't know—I just do. I don't like Sun. Do you know when I woke up the other day, the first thing I saw was her doing a headstand totally naked?"

Joni giggled. "You're kidding."

"Unfortunately not. That *fille* needs help. And I wouldn't trust her as far as I could throw her."

"I guess she does like attention, but I'm not worried," said Joni, looking worried. "She's been really nice to me. And I trust her."

I didn't say anything, just worked on the potatoes, putting mint and garlic around them and brushing them with olive oil.

"How did she look?" asked Joni.

"You don't want to know."

When everything was *finalement* ready in the dining room, Joni got Wolf from outside where he was smoking and I got Ms. G from upstairs. We poured them each a glass of wine and then put out the tray of canapés.

"This looks lovely, *kinder*," said Wolf, who was wearing his usual yoga pants, but with a very clean white poet shirt. "As do you, *ma chère* Emily." He pulled out her chair.

"Thank you, Wolf," said Ms. G.

"My pleasures."

Joni and I left the room and hid behind the door. We could hear Wolf and Ms. G talking quietly. I had hooked up my iPod to his stereo and it was playing my French dinner music softly in the background.

"This is just like *The Parent Trap*," I said, feeling nostalgic. "Remember when we watched that movie with Lindsay Lohan over and over again? Who knew that she'd end up in rehab and then gay?"

"I kind of wish they were our estranged parents," said Joni, looking at Ms. G and Wolf.

"Yeah, me too," I agreed. "And then we'd get to learn German, too."

We went back into the kitchen and I started preparing the chicken, pounding it thin per the recipe, dusting it with flour, and sautéing it in butter.

Joni was still fussing with the salad. "It wouldn't have mattered if I went with them anyway. I can't compete. Think about it: Sun's exotic, likes being naked, and has a fake ID."

"Joni, you've got a great figure too. And you're way smarter than Sun."

"Yeah, I guess. Could we not talk about her anymore? My stomach is hurting again."

"No *problème*." I wanted to ask Joni if she was still mad

at me, but since we were actually talking again, I was afraid to ruin things. She wasn't acting mad, but things were still really weird between us.

I turned the chicken over carefully and checked on the potatoes in the oven.

I couldn't help it. "Joni, are you still mad at me?"

She didn't respond.

"Do you want to talk about it?"

"No, I don't."

"Well, you're obviously still upset about it."

"No, I'm not." Joni was standing with her arms folded around her body, as if she was protecting herself.

"You're *so* not fine with it. I can tell by the way you're hunching up your shoulders."

Joni unwrapped her arms. "And what are you, the body language expert?"

"No, I just know you. Really well. I mean, we *have* been friends since third grade."

Joni grabbed some cucumbers and started chopping them roughly, not looking at me.

I leaned on the counter. "Do you still hate me?" I asked.

"I don't hate you. I just . . . look, I really don't want to talk about this, but since you started it. You knew how much I liked Sean. I mean, you listened to me talk about him, and you didn't say anything. You did stuff with him and didn't tell me."

"I wasn't trying to hurt you."

Joni kept chopping, hard, until little pieces of cucumber were spraying all over the place. "Well, you did. You knew I liked him, and you went ahead and kissed him and who knows what else. How could you do that?"

I picked a piece of cucumber out of my hair. "I'm sorry. I was wrong. I wasn't thinking. *Stupide moi*, I thought I was in love with him."

Joni stopped chopping. "Well, so did I. You know, if it had been the other way around, I would have told you how I felt. I would have told you everything."

I looked at her, even though she still wouldn't look at me. "I know I should have, but at first I thought you just had a little crush on him—that it wasn't serious—and then later, there was so much going on it just never seemed the right time to tell you. And when I did tell you, it was a disaster."

"I was so happy about him kissing me, and then to hear that he had done the same thing with you, can you imagine how I felt?" Joni glanced at me for a second and then looked away. Her face was turning all pink, like it always did when she got upset.

"No, it must have been awful."

"It was."

I tried to make a joke. "Did you ever get the henna out of the tiles?"

Joni almost smiled, and for a second I thought she might forgive me. "Yes, but it wasn't easy. I was so mad, Lotus."

"Are you going to be mad at me forever?"

"I don't know." Joni sighed deeply.

"It's totally over between me and him. You know that, right?"

"Uh-huh. But you should have told me. That was the

worst part. Not knowing what was going on. I felt . . ." Joni turned away from me and walked toward the refrigerator. I couldn't see her face but I could tell by her voice she was trying not to cry. "I felt . . . like an idiot!"

I walked after her. "I know. You're right. I should have told you. What happened. Everything."

Joni turned around and looked straight at me. I could see the tears in her eyes. "Yes, you should have."

"I'm sorry. I don't know what else to say. I'm sorry." I was beginning to feel hopeless again, like she was never going to forgive me.

Joni went back to examining the salads, cleaning off the edge of an already clean plate with a paper towel and then wiping her eyes with it. "It's just hard."

I felt like crying too. "You know, I've really missed you, Joni."

"Yeah, me too."

We stood there for a moment, silent, but no longer in that horrible, awkward way. It was an okay silence, as if we had released the tension into the air.

"I'm sorry that I didn't do anything for your birthday."

"It's okay."

Joni finally smiled, a tiny half-smile, and I knew things would be okay. "And thanks for coming back with me last night when I was sick. That was so embarrassing."

"*Pas de problème.* Hey, Joni, please don't get mad at me again, but you know, he's not really worth it."

Joni busied herself cleaning up the cucumber carnage. "I know that deep down. I just wanted to have a boyfriend."

"I know."

"Hey, Lotus, can I ask you something?"

"Sure."

"How far did you go, with Sean?"

I was so happy to be able to tell her that nothing really happened. "We just made out, that was it. What about you?"

"Pretty much the same. I mean, I guess we might have done more here in Montreal. But the first night Sun interrupted us, and last night I was too sick from *poutine*. And tonight . . . well, it didn't work out. Now I don't think I want to go any further."

"I know what you mean. So, are we okay?"

"I think so."

"Oh *merde*, my chicken." I ran to the stove and took it off the burner before it burned to a crisp. Then I poured in the champagne and some cream and stirred.

"Joni, could you taste this?"

Joni picked up a clean spoon and tasted the sauce. "Wow, Lotus, this is delicious. Seriously."

"Really? I've never made it before."

"Well, it's awesome."

I took out the potatoes and plated the chicken—that's what they say on all the cooking shows—and put some chopped parsley on top with a drizzle of sauce.

"Okay, let's go," I said to Joni. "And use a pot holder, it's hot."

Joni and I each took a plate and went into the living room. Wolf and Ms. G were leaning in toward each other, talking, their faces all glowy in the candlelight. Ornette Coleman was lying under the table. I could smell the lavender fragrance and the honey candles and the butter from the chicken, and I thought that it would make a nice perfume.

When we put down the plates, they said the chicken looked beautiful. Blushing modestly, we poured them some more wine and went back to the kitchen.

"They're so cute, aren't they?" said Joni, neatening up the kitchen.

"Adorable. They better invite us to the wedding."

Joni nodded. "But he's going to have to quit smoking first. Ms. G will never stand for that."

I whipped the cream for the dessert and put it on top of the chocolate cake I had bought at Première Moisson, my new favorite bakery in the world. Joni took a chocolate bar and made shavings to put on top, per my directions. We poured some of the grappa Sun had gotten into tiny little glasses and brought it out with the dessert.

"Hey, let's leave the lovebirds alone, okay?" I whispered to Joni.

"Good idea. Do you want to go out and get a coffee or something?"

"Sure."

We walked down the street to a little café with tables outside. I was so happy that Joni wasn't mad at me anymore. It was a beautiful night, warm with a slight breeze. We ate the little chocolates that came with our lattes and I thought about how much better they did everything in Montreal than in New York. There was just so much more care put into making everything special, like with the adorable little chocolates and the cute coffee cup.

"Hey, Joni, what do you think of that guy over there for me?" I pointed to one of those *canadiens typiques* with the long gray ponytail. He must have seen me looking at him, because he looked over and smiled and raised his eyebrows a little, as if we shared some dirty private joke. I winked and this made Joni and I start laughing uncontrollably, so bad that we had to leave the café. We walked back to the hostel, fantasizing about Ms. G and Wolf, whether we would walk in on them and what we should do.

"We'll just be really quiet and not look, you know, the way you don't look at your parents kissing," I said.

"My parents never kiss anyway," said Joni.

"I walked in on my father once. In the bathroom. Peeing," I said.

"Peeing and walking in on sex is a little different, don't you think?"

"Well, it was *très* traumatizing. He tried to have a talk with me about it, but I pretended I didn't know what he was talking about."

We walked in the door, quiet as mice.

"I think I hear something," whispered Joni.

We crept inside and saw them, two shapes entwined on the couch, kissing and sighing and making those little moany noises. I heard someone giggle and, as my eyes adjusted to the darkness, I realized that the girl on the couch wasn't Ms. G, but Sun. And she wasn't with Wolf, but with Sean. I grabbed Joni, who was behind me, and we ran to the kitchen.

"That was them, wasn't it?" said Joni. She was shaking

and her eyes were all wide. "Sean and Sun! Do you think they saw us?"

"No," I said, thinking that they were totally focused on each other.

Joni opened the refrigerator and grabbed all the leftovers from dinner and breakfast as well as other food I hadn't seen before, spreading it all out on the counter. There were three kinds of cheeses, pumpernickel bread and the thick slab of butter, leftover chicken, dill pickles, olives, cheese straws, and pastries. Joni took a piece of pumpernickel and slathered butter on it and then cut a hunk of cheese and put it on top.

"Are you okay?" I said, looking at the food she was about to consume.

"I will be," she said, taking a big bite. It seemed to calm her down, because she had stopped shaking.

I cut a piece of cheese into tiny pieces. "That hypocrite, her and her Buddhist philosophy," I said, feeling furious.

"You were right about her," said Joni.

"I'm not happy about it or anything."

"I know."

Joni took some ham out of the refrigerator and piled it on her sandwich, taking another big bite. "Life sucks. My mother is sick. My father is not around. My so-called boyfriend is a cheater."

I didn't know what to say. "Well, at least this cheese is really good."

Joni took another bite. "Yeah, what do you think it is, Gruyère?"

"Yeah, or maybe one of those artisanal Canadian cheeses. Watch out, it could be unpasteurized."

"I don't even care. You know, that's all you can count on in life, things like cheese and bread."

"Yeah."

"I hope she gets pregnant."

"Or an STD."

"I hope they both get one. And the worst part is, I know what he would say if I confronted him."

"Yeah, something like 'I need to be free' or 'I can't be tied down' . . . all that crap."

Joni nodded.

"Well, we're leaving tomorrow, so at least we won't have to see her anymore."

We stayed in the kitchen and ate leftovers until we were too tired and stuffed to eat another bite.

"Do you think they're still out there?" asked Joni.

"I don't know, it's awfully quiet. Maybe they heard us and left. We haven't been that quiet."

We opened the door to the main room, but the sofa was empty. Next, we went to Women Lounging. Ms. G and Sun were lying on their futons sleeping (or pretending to sleep) as if nothing had happened, as if it had all been a dream.

"Let's put a hex on her," I whispered.

Joni nodded. I waved my arms around Sun's head and whispered, "You are now forever and ever cursed and nothing good will ever happen to you again. Wicca Wicca Wicca. Everything you touch will turn to sand, and every boy you meet will find you hideous. Wicca Wicca Wicca. Amen."

In the middle of the night, I went to the kitchen to get some water. Sun was there, eating an apple, wearing a T-shirt that said BODY BY POUTINE and thong underpants.

"You're unbelievable," I said.

Sun looked slightly embarrassed.

"You know, Joni thought you were her friend. She trusted you. Do you think it's nice to fool around with someone else's boyfriend? Isn't that going to create some bad karma?"

"You should know." Sun took a big bite of the apple. "Joni told me you had a thing with Sean and she's your best friend. Or was."

"Stop it. That's irrelevant and it doesn't excuse you from doing this right in front of her."

"We thought you guys were asleep."

"Well, we weren't."

Sun started doing little ballet moves, using the kitchen counter as a barre.

"Could you stop that? It's really annoying."

Sun shrugged. "Whatever. Anyway, shouldn't you be talking to Sean? He's the one you're really mad at."

I turned and left the kitchen. I guess she was right. About one thing. I was angry with Sean. But what was the point of talking to him? He had already made clear his stupid free-love philosophy and how he couldn't be tied down blah blah blah, so if Joni was with him, she knew what to expect. But even if someone tells you how they are, it can still make you mad that that's how they are. You keep thinking you're going to be the one to change them. I went back to sleep cursing Sean and Sun in my mind.

fifteen

Dernier jour in Montreal

"I'm thinking about staying in Montreal for a while," Sean announced as we sat down to breakfast.

"You're kidding," I said.

"That would be cool," said Sun, drinking some kefir, this weird yogurt drink.

Joni tried to look like she didn't care, but she looked more like she was trying not to cry. I tried to send more evil spells Sun's way, but they didn't seem to have any effect, because she wasn't showing any signs of getting the plague.

Sun left the table to take a shower. Joni left soon after to go pack. Sean looked like he was going to follow her, so I said, "Why don't you leave her alone? That way, she can get over you."

"I just want to stay here in Montreal, it's not about . . ." He looked at the door where Joni and Sun had gone. "This is just something I want to do. For me."

"Right, this has nothing to do with last night, and I'm sure your parents are going to be thrilled! Maybe you could quit school and get a job making *poutine*."

"Lotus, what's your problem?"

"My problem is you," I said. "You call yourself an existentialist, but you're really a selfish jerk. I thought you were really deep, but you don't try to face the existential void at all! All you want to do is have a good time with whoever is around, and the thing is, I really liked you, maybe even loved you."

Sean looked stunned. "But—"

"Don't say anything." I grabbed the half-empty bottle of kefir and threw it in the trash. "I'm sick to death of your apologies, but next time, and I'm sure there will be a *prochaine fois*, try to think of the other person's feelings a little bit."

Sean was tapping his foot nervously. "Look, Lotus, you knew how I felt. I didn't pretend. I told you that I couldn't have a serious relationship."

"I knew, but I still got hurt. And Joni got hurt. And for all I know, Portia got hurt."

Sean looked miserable. "I wasn't trying to hurt anyone. I just wanted to be free, like J.P."

"Well, maybe you could try to be free without hurting

people. And I'm not sure J.P. was right about that whole free-love thing. I'm getting more into Kierkegaard now anyway. He said that love is all."

Before Sean had a chance to respond, Ms. G and Wolf arrived at the table with plates piled high with buckwheat crêpes doused with butter and gooseberry jam. They hadn't noticed anything that was going on, because they had been at the stove cooking, totally involved with each other.

"Since you made us dinner last night, we wanted to make you *kinder* a special breakfast," said Wolf.

"Thanks, that's really sweet."

"Yeah, thanks," said Sean.

Wolf made a coffee toast to our departure. "It's *auf Wiedersehen*, but not farewell or goodbye. You know, I'm thinking of making a change myself. The hostel business, she not so good right now, you know, and I have a cousin in the Red Hook of the Brooklyn, and he wants to open a beer hall, boccie court, and Internet café. He is always asking my help."

"Wow, that would be great," I said, and Ms. G blushed. Sean just kept eating his crêpes and being quiet.

During our third cup of coffee, Sun came back with a towel around her head and scarfed down a crêpe. In the middle of her second crêpe, her cell phone rang and she started talking to someone, sounding more Valley Girl than ever. "I'm psyched. That's awesome. I love you." When she hung up the phone, she tried to hug me, but I resisted.

She was practically jumping up and down. "I just got some great news. My boyfriend's just finished the Ironman in Finland and he's coming here tonight! You're all going to love him." She was so excited, it was nauseating. I guess she had already forgotten that we were leaving.

Sean was in the middle of eating his fourth crêpe as she said this and he started to choke so hard that Wolf had to pat him on the back.

I turned to Sun. "What about that thing in your Buddhist book about not trying to be the fastest? Aren't triathlons all about being the fastest?"

"Oh, he's not competitive or anything, he just competes against himself."

"Brilliant strategy," I said sarcastically. "I'll have to try that."

I brought Joni a crêpe in the Women Lounging but she didn't want to eat, or talk. "I don't care what Sean does," she said. "I just want to go home."

Gare (Train Station)

When Ms. G heard about Sean's plan to stay in Montreal, she said there was no way she was letting him stay unsupervised or travel home on his own. He actually seemed a little relieved to be forced to go back with us. After our conversation, he was being especially nice to me, but I didn't really care anymore.

I walked around the station, feeling restless. Joni and Sean were huddled in the corner of the waiting room, talking. The way Joni was shaking her head, it didn't look good for Sean.

Ms. G was on the phone with Wolf, so I decided to go get a latte. As I drank it, I jotted down a few thoughts. As J.P. says, for an occurrence to become an adventure, it is necessary and sufficient for one to recount it.

Pensées de Gare (Thoughts While in the Train Station)

Joni and I are reconciled, which is *merveilleux*. I feel like a huge weight has been lifted from me.

My French has not improved, but it's probably just as well—I want to keep my Parisian accent pure. People speak French here in Montreal, but other than that, it's really a lot like New York, except there are better pastries and more public bathrooms. Maybe next time, I need to immerse myself in a culture where people speak no English at all.

After the success of last night's dinner, I am thinking of becoming a chef, although I'm not sure white is my best color.

I am feeling very disillusioned about love, *après* Sean, but seeing Ms. G and Wolf, I guess there's at least hope. Still, I think I'll remain single—at least for ten or twenty more years.

Strangely, I am looking forward to going home.

After my café break, I walked by a Chapters. I saw a sign in the window about a reading for Mireille's new book. I looked more closely and saw the reading was today, at two o'clock, but since it was already four o'clock, no doubt it was over. *Merde, merde,* and *double merde.*

I went into the bookstore anyway. In the back, several employees were packing up *French Women for All Seasons,* and then I saw a woman chatting with one of the bookstore people. I looked again.

It was her, Mireille, the author of *FWDGF,* in the flesh!

I walked over and stood in front of her, speechless, feeling like an idiot. One of the bookstore girls said, "Hello, I'm sorry you missed the reading, but if you want a book, we can get a signed one for you." And then, like in a movie, Mireille looked up at me and said, *"Bonjour."*

Words spilled out of my mouth. "OhmyGod. *Ohmon-Dieu.* I have all your books. I love your books. I live by your books. I've written you letters. And I'm a member of your Web site, too," I lied.

"Bon, bon," she said, smiling a little, probably trying to decide if I was dangerous or not.

Mireille looked like one of those people who could pack for a month in a tiny carry-on and never look wrinkled. She was wearing all gray, a soft gray sweater and darker gray slacks. Even her hair was a beautiful silvery blond.

"This is amazing. You are my hero. You and Christiane Amanpour."

She laughed then, a silvery gray laugh, as if she had decided I was harmless.

"And what is your name? *Comment vous appelez-vous?"*

I couldn't remember a word of French. "Uh, my name, *mon nom est Lotus,"* I blurted out.

"C'est charmant."

"Merci. Thank you."

"And how does it go, with the book?"

I couldn't believe she was actually interested in *moi.* "It's great. I haven't had much success with the yogurt, probably because I don't have a yogurt maker, but I've made a bunch of other *recettes* from your book. Like last night, I made the chicken—le chicken au champagne—and *tout le monde* loved it."

"That's wonderful. I make that all the time *chez moi.* Ah

yes, the yogurt maker—*c'est un problème*. You need to buy one, and you must have one made in France, *bien sûr*."

"That must have been the problem."

"*Oui*. So, let me look at you. You have chic like a French woman. The way you put together an ensemble."

"*Merci*." I looked down proudly at my purple leggings and black and white tunic.

The bookstore girls were hovering around us, packing up the books.

Mireille picked up her Hermès bag.

"I guess it's time to go," I said, kind of sad.

"*Alors*, I have a little time before my train. You want a coffee? You have the time?"

"Yes, of course, I mean *oui*. My friend Joni likes to get everywhere super early."

"*Les Américains sont fous*—you know, crazy. But *quand même*, they like my book, *alors* . . ." Mireille shrugged.

We ducked into a little restaurant with white modular chairs that went really well with my outfit. A waiter appeared as soon as we sat down. "Ladies?"

"*J'ai changé d'avis*. I've changed my mind. I think I must have champagne. You have Veuve Clicquot?" asked Mireille.

The waiter looked sad. "I'm so sorry."

"*Pas de problème*, Domaine Chandon will have to do."

She looked at me. "And for the young lady, your best sparkling apple cider, *s'il vous plaît*. If you were French, I could give you champagne, but given *les moeurs* of your puritan country, I think we better not chance it. Oh, and some *mousse au chocolat*, please."

"Right away." The waiter disappeared.

"So, tell me about yourself, Lotus."

"Well, I used to be an existentialist, but it didn't really work out. Now I want to be a journalist."

"Writing, that's wonderful, but why did you give up on philosophy?"

"You know, I had it all figured out. I was going to be an existentialist, move to France, fall in love, and be free. But then I fell for someone who was a little too free, if you know what I mean, never made it to France, and almost lost my best friend. I guess I'm a failed existentialist."

"There is no such thing. You had a *crise, c'est tout*, that's all, an existential crisis, but that does not mean you should give up."

The waiter brought her a glass of champagne and me a small bottle of pink sparkling cider, which he poured into a champagne glass. I felt very elegant and sophisticated.

I drank my cider in a single gulp.

Mireille picked up her glass. "Lotus, when you drink champagne, or in your case, sparkling cider, you must savor it. That is the key. That's what I'm talking about in the book. And that is what existentialism is about. This moment. This drink. That's all there is. I want you to remember this."

I nodded.

"So, you want to be a *journaliste*. That's very interesting. I'm actually thinking about writing a new book: *French Teens Don't Get Fat*. And, I think *peut-être* you may be able to help me."

"*Moi?* That would be *incroyable*. But how could I help?"

"You could be my American correspondent. You could e-mail me what is going on with teenagers in the States. How they feel about their bodies. You, for example. You did the *régime* from my book, yes? How did it work for you?"

"To be *complètement* honest, I didn't lose any weight."

At that moment, the waiter brought the *mousse au chocolat* and two spoons.

Mireille handed me a spoon. "Here, dig in, as you say."

I hesitated. I didn't want her to think I was a piggy *Américaine*.

Mireille put the spoon in my hand. "Lotus, have some mousse. You must enjoy life! Eat chocolate. This is what I'm talking about. If you deny yourself, you will be unhappy. But if you allow yourself these small pleasures, then you will not feel deprived and binge on the fast food."

I took a bite. I couldn't believe it. Here I was eating chocolate mousse with Mireille of *FWDGF*. I couldn't wait to tell Joni. She wasn't going to believe it.

As I took another spoonful of chocolate mousse, savoring the dark velvety taste of it, I realized that if I hadn't gone through all this drama—my heart getting stomped on by Sean, almost losing Joni forever, and even doubting J.P.— I wouldn't be sitting here with Mireille, getting ready to start my new life as a teen lifestyle reporter. I immediately saw myself in a cute gold trench coat and high heels, holding a large microphone, interviewing teen celebrities, and reporting back to Mireille in Paris. I envisioned her on TV, interviewing for her new book, *French Teens Don't Get Fat*, and telling Oprah how she couldn't have done it all without Lotus Lowenstein.

Mireille smiled. "It's good, yes?"

"Yes, *très bonne*."

"*Exactement*. It's not about weight, Lotus, it's about lifestyle, enjoying life, not rushing through it."

I nodded, agreeing.

Mireille motioned for more champagne.

I protested, "But in the book you say to have only one glass."

Mireille shrugged again. "Oh, the book, pff. Lotus, it is very important to break the rules, *les règles*, now and then. And to seriously discuss *l'existentialisme*, I believe, calls for a *deuxième* glass of champagne. So, go on with your story, you were telling me about your experiences. Have you read *Le Deuxième Sexe?*"

"*Oui*. Yes, I loved it."

"And Sartre?"

"Of course."

The waiter brought her a second glass of champagne and poured the rest of my cider into my glass.

"So, what happened?" asked Mireille, leaning forward.

"Well, there was a boy . . ."

"*Bien sûr*, there is always a boy. And . . . ?"

We clinked our glasses and I began to tell my story.

Libby Schmais

is the author of the adult novels *The Perfect Elizabeth* and *The Essential Charlotte*. *The Pillow Book of Lotus Lowenstein* is her first novel for young readers. She lives in Brooklyn, New York.